WALK THE BLOODY BOULEVARD

Walk the Bloody Boulevard

A. A. MARCUS

WILDSIDE PRESS

WALK THE BLOODY BOULEVARD

1

PETER HUNTER even *looked* like a private detective. His nose was crooked and the thin lips beneath it ironed themselves into a hard twisted mouth. His eyes were frosty, the pale blue of polar ice. His face was tautly impassive.

He coiled his long lean body into a leather chair like a man winding up a spring. He leaned back, relaxed, but it was as though he could strike out with tremendous power at any moment.

He turned a brusque stare at George Kennedy. In the utter frigidity of those eyes was conveyed the suggestion that any formalities would be wasted.

George Kennedy leaned forward. "I want a man found," he said.

Hunter nodded. He said nothing.

"I hear you're good," Kennedy said.

Again, Hunter nodded.

Kennedy said, "This is urgent—"

"It always is," Hunter snapped. "Whether it's a poodle or a blonde, it's always life-and-death. Let's get to the point."

Kennedy frowned. He was a big good-looking man with a decisive manner about him. Now, he said, "I want quick results. If you find my man in three days, I'll pay a thousand dollar bonus."

"Who is he?"

"A man named Williams. Samuel Williams."

"Missing how long?"

"Two days."

"What do the police say?"

"I don't know. I haven't consulted them."

"Why not?"

Kennedy hesitated. Hunter's eyes narrowed suspiciously at the delay.

"I want faster action than the police can give," Kennedy said finally.

Hunter said nothing. There was a moment of silence.

For the first time, Kennedy noticed Hunter's hands. They possessed a vibrancy, an aliveness like that of an independent organism. The fingers were long and slim and wiry. They drummed impatiently on the arm of the chair, then stopped, curved tensely in mid-air.

As though they were sensitive to the very atmosphere of the room. Sifting it . . . Appraising it . . .

The fingers gnarled themselves into a fist. "Give me all the facts," he said. The words tumbled out of his mouth flatly. Take-this-or-leave-it, they seemed to say. "You Engineers like to *look* efficient. You even leave things out so you can look that way. Right now, it's more important to be thorough."

Kennedy reddened. He clenched his big square hands. "If this wasn't so important—" he flared.

"Yes."

"I'd tell you to go to hell."

8

Hunter's thin lips grinned humorlessly. "All right—you've told me." He waved an expressive hand. "Now, say something constructive."

Kennedy tensed stiffly, feet flat to the floor, square hands gripping the arms of the chair. His jaw jutted angrily. His furious eyes stabbed Hunter, then shifted to the door.

Peter Hunter leaned back in the chair, apparently indifferent to Kennedy's ultimate decision. But the vibrant fingers, cupped and waiting, belied the indolent draping of the lean body.

He looked around the office like a man measuring an opponent. It was quietly luxurious: the massive walnut desk . . . the expensive gray carpeting . . . the yellow leather couch. It was all very dignified, yet quite modern.

Abruptly Kennedy leaned forward. He clasped his hands on the desk. Even before he began to speak, a quick gleam of triumph burned briefly in Hunter's eyes.

"Samuel Williams," George Kennedy said, "was the city's chief highway chemist for the past twenty years. He was fussy, precise, extremely efficient—"

"He's retired?" Hunter interrupted.

"No."

"Dead, then."

"*Dead?*" Kennedy frowned.

Hunter's lips sharpened to a knife edge. "You speak of him in the past tense." His eyes bored deep into the engineer's.

Kennedy's eyes curtained. "I don't know," he said wonderingly. "I'm not sure." He shook his head. "Yes, it is odd that I should have spoken like that."

"Go on." Hunter's fingers seemed to tighten into talons.

"Williams phoned me at the office day before yesterday—Monday, that would be. He was quite excited. Insisted he

9

had to see me. I invited him to the office. He refused. Said he didn't want to be seen coming to me. I suggested my suite at the hotel. He agreed, reluctantly"

"And then?"

"I never saw him."

"He didn't come."

"No."

"What hotel?"

"The Scott."

"You live there?"

"Yes."

"Go on."

"Next day I called his wife. She was frantic—he'd left home Monday night and never returned. She notified the police. I asked my lawyer about a private detective. He recommended you."

Hunter leaned back. Thin lips plumed cigarette smoke at the ceiling. The electric fingers rubbed against each other. As though the story was a fabric—and they were seeking flaws in its weave.

He jerked himself erect. "What did this Williams have," he asked sharply, "that was so infernally hot?"

Again, Kennedy hesitated. Hunter's thin mouth twitched. The sensitive fingers tensed.

Easily, the engineer said, "Oh, just a campaign matter. I'm running for mayor, you know."

"I know." Hunter's shrug was indifferent. "Why should he slink about it?"

Kennedy's answer was glib. "He didn't want his office to know he was working with me. They're all for Burkett—my opponent—down there."

Hunter shook his head. "His wife can't explain the disappearance?"

"She's dumbfounded."

10

"Another woman, maybe?"

Kennedy's smile was good-humored. "Williams was almost seventy. He hadn't looked at another woman for fifty years."

The thin lips twisted. The voice became sharply ironical. "Some guys don't have to look," Hunter said softly. "They dream. For years and years, they dream. Then one day . . . a pair of lush lips smiles at them . . . and they wake up. They start running—after the first chippy they see."

"No."

"You're sure?"

"Not Williams."

Hunter shrugged. He looked down at his expressive hands. They curled into fists, opened again. He thrust them into his pockets. As though to get them out of the way.

He stood up. "I get a hundred a day. Plus expenses. I get a week in advance."

He watched as Kennedy wrote the check. "The bonus still goes," Kennedy said easily. He signed his name with a flourish. "Three days. A thousand dollars."

Kennedy handed him the check. Hunter took it, turned to go. At the door, he stopped. "While I'm gone," he said softly, "see if you can't recall the *real* reason Williams was so anxious to see you."

Then, as Kennedy flushed angrily, he stepped out of the office.

Out in the street, he looked down at the folded check, still in his hand. The thin lips parted in a grim smile that bared sharp wolf-like teeth.

He turned his frozen eyes up to the windows of the offices of Kennedy and Blake, Engineering Consultants.

"You lousy liar," he growled, under his breath. "You poor . . . lousy . . . inefficient . . . liar!"

2

TWO HOURS later that day, at noon, Peter Hunter was back in his office. Tim Moloney, his close friend and partner, was at a cabinet, pouring out two shots of rye.

He took one and handed it to Hunter. He draped his splintery six feet three inches into an uncomfortable wooden armchair. He sipped his drink. He sighed.

"We're working," Hunter said.

Moloney ran his free hand through a shock of blond hair. He waited for an explanation.

"Give me a rundown on a guy named George Kennedy."

Tim's eyebrows lifted. "*The* George Kennedy."

"That's right."

"The mayoralty candidate?"

"The same. Our client."

"Our client?"

"Since this morning."

Moloney frowned.

"Stop stalling," Hunter snapped.

13

Moloney grimaced. Hunter leaned forward intently. His hands stretched expectantly.

"Full name—George Palmer Kennedy," Tim said. "An only child. Both parents dead. Born with a silken diaper on his fanny. Old family. Ooodles and Oodles of ough-day. Bachelor. No permanent female associations. Lives at the Scott." Tim stopped to sort out facts in his mind. "Top-notch engineer. Organized Kennedy and Blake, Engineering Consultants, before the war. Good firm. Highly thought of in the trade."

"Military service?"

"Colonel, Engineers. Spent the war in Burma, building supply roads through the jungle."

"What about his politics?"

"He says," Tim paused, then repeated the words with emphasis, "he *says* he's out to get the vets a square deal. Decent housing and that sort of thing."

"You don't believe him?"

"I don't believe anyone."

"Who's his backer?"

Tim put his fingers to his nose. "Mike Wyatt."

"That crook."

"Mike put Harlan Burkett, the present mayor, into office. But Burkett got stiff-necked, flouted Mike on patronage, began to build his own machine. Mike saw to it that Burkett didn't get the party nomination this time. So Burkett thumbed his nose at Mike and took his new machine into the opposition party. Now, he's *their* candidate."

"Gentlemen of high principle," Hunter said drily.

Hunter pressed his cruel lips together. "What about Kennedy—what kind of guy is he?"

Moloney didn't answer.

"What I mean is—do you figure him honest?"

14

Tim's grin was sour. " 'To be honest is nothing: the repu-tation of it is all,' " he quoted.

"Spare me the erudition," Hunter rasped. "Is he straight or a conniver?" His hands clenched. "How far can I trust him?"

The skinny man's grin vanished. "All I have is a hunch."

"Give."

"When Kennedy began this campaign, he scared the right people. He lambasted the police as corrupt. He was going to get housing."

"Sounds good."

"He promised to fight for repeal of the county dry laws."

"Fine."

"He was going to run the bookies out of town."

"Well?"

"But what happens? Under cover, the bookies contribute to his campaign fund. The realty boys back him—and you know how they *love* municipal housing. And every speak-easy in town has his picture—and how long would they last without dry laws?"

"They think Kennedy's lying?"

"Those boys don't think. They *know*."

"How?"

"The word is out. He'll play ball."

"Who put the word out?"

Moloney grimaced. "Mike Wyatt."

"Why he?"

"They wouldn't take it from anyone else. They know Mike. He's pulled crooked deals for them before."

Hunter fell silent. His cold blue eyes stared at the ceiling: the sharp lips ironed themselves down to a razor edge; the slim quick fingers strained against each other.

Abruptly, he launched into a résumé of his meeting with

15

Kennedy. His voice was low, his face impassive. Moloney listened carefully, then said, "How do you figure it?"

"He's lying," Hunter said. "I'm sure of that. It was more than just a campaign matter. I don't know if Williams is missing or—"

"Or what?"

"Or if he's running away from Kennedy?"

"What do *I* do?"

"*You* get on Kennedy's tail right now. I want to know who he sees, where he goes, what he does—the works."

"And you?"

Hunter held up two stiff fingers. "I got two things to do. First, to look for Samuel Williams."

"Ar.d?"

"Second—to make sure Kennedy isn't pulling a fast one."

The skinny blond cocked his head to a side uncertainly. "What if he is? What's it to you?"

Hunter's answer was a strangling gesture of his sinewy fingers.

Tim said, sarcastically: "I think your conscience is beginning to show."

Hunter tightened his lips. He said nothing.

"Why can't we go along playing footsie with him? At a hundred bucks a day, what do you care if he's on the level or not? What are you—a Galahad?"

"Lay off, Tim."

Moloney persisted. "The trouble with you, Pete—"

Hunter jerked his head up at the sound of his first name. "I said: 'Lay off!' " he snapped.

"Not till I've finished. You're still carrying that miserable sense of guilt about the crack-up in Italy you went through during the war. You're trying to appease it by playing the social avenger. You don't give a goddam about Williams any

16

more. You've decided Kennedy's a crook and you're out to get him."

"Through, Tim?" Hunter asked softly. "Are you through?"

"Why don't you smarten up, Pete? If people get fooled, it's because they don't care. And if they don't give a good goddam, then why in hell should you?"

"Maybe you're right, Timmy. Maybe you're right." He looked down at his hands, then lifted his head so that he could look directly into his partner's eyes. His voice came out in a snarl. "But I spent four years in the army. I'd hate to think I was helping some cheap crook to make suckers out of the guys who were my buddies."

There was silence for a moment. Then Tim got up and came around behind the desk. He put his face very close to Hunter's.

"You know who you're up against?"

"I know, Timmy. I know."

"Mike Wyatt. He's Mr. Big around here. He's had more guys killed than you got teeth in your mouth." His voice sharpened. "He'd rub you like a flea if you endangered him."

"I know it."

"There was a guy named Joe Samuels, remember him? He uncovered the dirt on that crooked sewer job. He had Mike on the ropes, was going to force a prosecution. He left a fine widow, didn't he?"

Hunter shrugged.

Tim threw up his hands. "Okay, I did my best. I know you. You're going through with it."

Hunter met his eyes. "You knew I would, didn't you?"

"Yes, I knew it. Because I know you. But, dammit, I had to try." He threw his arm around Hunter's shoulder. "Okay, where do we begin?"

17

Hunter's face softened. His grin was warm. He said: "I knew you'd come along for the ride, Timmy. I knew it all the time."

Tim said: "I'm tired of living, anyway."

At nine that evening, Moloney called in to report. The skinny blond man said he had leeched onto George Kennedy immediately after lunch. The engineer had gone to the offices of the Barclay Construction Company.

"He was there only five minutes," Tim said, "but he came out looking like a guy who'd been eviscerated. Dead white."

"And after that?"

"Spent the afternoon at his office, ate dinner at his hotel. Drove out to the Barclay mansion at eight. At eight forty, the first prowl car arrived."

Hunter's hands tightened. "Prowl car."

"One of the drivers was a friend of mine. Told me Barclay blew his brains out."

"Suicide!" The knuckles showed white on the hand that gripped the receiver. "With Kennedy in the house?"

"Far as I know, he's still in the house."

"The cops are *sure* it's a suicide?"

"If they think otherwise," Moloney said drily, "they're not confiding in me."

"Stay with it. Check that suicide angle."

"What if Kennedy leaves?"

"Follow him."

There was a short pause before Moloney asked, "This case is fogging up, isn't it? A highway chemist disappears. A highway contractor blows his top. How do you figure it?"

Hunter's laugh was grim. "I don't figure it, Timmy. I'm just going along for the ride." He hung up.

18

Walk the Bloody Boulevard

Hunter dressed, went out to his car. The night was gray and dark. A fugitive moon fled from cloud to cloud, alternately flooding the street with its brilliance, then leaving it draped in ominous shadow.

Hunter drove downtown, parked his gray coupe a block from the Municipal Building, then walked back to the huge skyscraper. He stopped across the street from it, staring up at the rows of empty black windows.

He went around the corner to the entrance. There, he stood, peering in at the silent darkness. The lobby was a huge square divided into two smaller rectangles by a corridor which crossed it. Beyond the corridor, in the rear rectangle, were the banks of elevators.

Hunter eased the lobby door shut behind him. Only one elevator was in service at this hour of the night. A yellow square of light shone out of its cage.

He slid along the dark shadow of the wall until he reached the intersecting corridor, turned into it and followed it to the fire stairs. The heavy door opened soundlessly. He started up the stairs.

Dim safety bulbs on the landings shed the only light. At the fourth floor, he opened the heavy steel fire door and entered into the hall off of which were located the offices.

He stood absolutely still. Waiting. The long fingers of his hands extended themselves into the darkness. They seemed to tremble. Like the searching antennae of a predatory insect—alert to the slightest vibration of danger.

Hunter moved down the hall. At each office door, he stopped to shine his pencil flash on the frosted pane. At the one marked, CHEMIST, he smiled.

Once inside the office of Samuel Williams, Hunter held his breath. The pupils of his straining eyes dilated; they seemed to stab their way through the black. Finally, satisfied

19

he was alone and unfollowed, he switched on the pencil flash, flicked its beam around the room.

An outmoded handset telephone rested on an old rolltop desk. Half a dozen wooden file-cases hugged the wall. Hunter's avid hands yanked the drawer of the first open.

The thin beam of the pencil flash stabbed quickly across yellowed old documents, written in a flowing Spencerian hand. Hunter leaned closer, then shook his head and closed the drawer.

Suddenly he stiffened.

From out in the hall came the barely audible sound of a muffled footstep.

He slithered to the door, placed himself so that he would be behind it when it swung open.

On the frosted pane, a bulky shadow loomed. Hunter drew a deep silent breath.

In the darkness the cold blue eyes seemed afire. The quick fingers stole to the shoulder holster. When they came out again, they were wrapped around an automatic.

The knob turned. The figure materialized. It stepped into the office. Smoothly, without hurry, Hunter sledged the butt of the gun down on the newcomer's skull.

The man pitched forward. His head hit the floor with a thump.

The thin beam of the flash stabbed at the intruder's face. Shock widened Hunter's cold eyes. His clenched fist jerked open.

He bent over the unconscious man. The long thin fingers went through the man's pockets. The wallet was fat and well-filled. He looked at the papers, counted the money, then returned them.

In the side pocket of the jacket, the sensitive fingers found a business card. On its reverse side was a message, written in a neat handwriting. It said:

20

Walk the Bloody Boulevard

Williams, the highway chemist, says the cylinders on the Belt Boulevard job were deficient. We ought to talk it over before something drastic happens.

K.

He turned the torch back to the fallen man. He crouched, lifted one eyelid and stared into the vacant pupil. He let the eyelid fall shut.

He put the card back into the jacket pocket, then stood erect. The electric fingers closed in the characteristic gesture of strangulation.

He went to the door and paused there before leaving. Once more, he flicked the light to the face of the man on the floor.

The unconscious man was his client—George Kennedy.

Hunter closed the door softly.

"All I know about last night," Tim said, as they ate breakfast the following morning, "is that Kennedy left the Barclay mansion about nine thirty. He drove straight downtown to the Municipal building and sneaked inside. I couldn't follow. I'd be wide open in there. I waited about half an hour. Then you came out and told me to beat it. I beat it."

"Nobody tailed you?"

"Nobody."

Hunter nodded and turned his attention to THE SENTINEL's front-page story of the death of Harrison Barclay. It admitted no other possibility but suicide. The obit on the inside pages spoke glowingly of the deceased's achievements as president of the Barclay Construction Corporation.

His most recent accomplishment had been the building of the multi-million dollar Belt Boulevard, completed only last month, which had been so spectacularly successful in

21

reducing accidents and eliminating traffic congestion on the city's business streets.

Nowhere—neither in the news account nor in the obit—was George Kennedy's name mentioned.

Hunter put the paper down and produced pictures of Samuel Williams. "Take a couple of these and try to back-track on Williams's movements the night he disappeared. Start with the bus drivers. The guy doesn't have a car so he must have used some public transportation. Buses, cabs—you know the pitch."

The skinny blond nodded, put the pictures in his pocket. He eyed his partner narrowly. "What do you make of it so far?"

Hunter's sharp teeth vexed his thin lip. "A lot of pieces . . . but they don't make a pattern yet." He extended tight fingers, began to tick them off. "A missing chemist . . . a contractor's suicide . . . a skulking candidate for mayor . . . Politics . . . liquor . . . Mike Wyatt . . ." He clenched the fingers into a fist. He grinned humorlessly. "They don't fit. Let's try to find some more pieces."

3

AFTER TIM had left, Hunter finished his breakfast and drove to the offices of THE SENTINEL. There, he spent an hour poring over old issues of the newspaper, studying clippings about the recently-completed Belt Boulevard.

At ten thirty, he left the newspaper office and drove downtown, parking before a large apartment hotel. He sat in the car for about five minutes smoking a cigarette. Finally, he threw the cigarette away and went into the building.

An elevator took him up to the eighth floor. He walked down the hall, knocked on the door of the last apartment in the corridor.

The door opened warily. A bespectacled, baby-faced balding man in disheveled blue pajamas peered out at him.

"You're Westrope?"

The baby-faced man nodded.

Hunter brushed past him into the suite. "I tried to get you at your office. They told me you closed up. My name's Hunter. Peter Hunter."

"And just what is the nature of your business with me,

23

Mr. Hunter?" He spoke in a high tenor, and his enunciation was elegant to the point of affectation.

The detective didn't answer. His sharp eyes stabbed their way around the room. There was an ornately carved sofa, upholstered in a lustrous brocade. The walls were hung with what seemed to be tapestried scenes from the Decameron. Two small gilt chairs, their backs harp-shaped, stood on spindly legs in the center of a luxurious Oriental rug. They looked very elegant—and very uncomfortable.

Hunter crossed to the bookcase. The volumes on the shelves made him lift his eyebrows: Freud, Havelock Ellis, Frank Harris, D. H. Lawrence, the Kinsey Report . . .

He drew a deep breath. "Whew! Are these part of the furnishings? Do they come with the joint, Westrope?"

"They happen to be mine."

There was a note of pride in Westrope's voice. Hunter turned to look at him. The baby-faced chemist met his stare with a frown that gave his childish features a petulant expression.

"You don't look very smoky to me," Hunter said. "Still—" he shrugged "—you never know where the fires are burning."

The baby-faced man colored. "I see nothing remarkable in a man's concern with what is admittedly the most important aspect of human behavior."

"Purely academic, eh?" The question was a taunt.

"Ah—exactly."

Hunter took a large, thin, leather-bound, gold-tooled volume. He let it fall open at random. The page disclosed an enlarged picture of a naked woman, her body lewdly distorted.

"And where," the detective asked sourly, "does this fit in?"

"That is *art!*"

"Smut, you mean. The stuff they hide under the counter from the cops." His eloquent fingers managed to convey

24

disgust as they returned the book to its shelf. "You're supposed to outgrow this sort of thing."

Westrope's fingers dug through his thinning hair furiously. The hands were soft and pudgy. A large diamond nestled brightly among the folds of flesh. The nails were polished a soft pink.

"Is this what you came to see me about?" he choked.

Hunter stared at him. His brow furrowed in the effort to analyze the little man, to fit him into an understandable category. "Say," he asked suddenly, "you're not in the business, are you? Peddling this filth, I mean?"

Westrope strode to the door. "I'm afraid I shall have to ask you to leave."

"Not before you talk to me about an old guy named Samuel Williams," Hunter said sharply.

"Williams!" Westrope froze. A petulant frown creased his smooth face. "I don't know anyone by that name."

"I thought you chemists all knew each other."

"Oh—you mean the Williams who was chemist at the Highway Department."

"I don't mean the one who settled Rhode Island."

Obviously nettled, Westrope produced a cork-tipped cigarette. He made a great ceremony of lighting it.

Hunter sniffed at the smoke. "Perfumed, no less," he exclaimed incredulously.

"The finer things in life, Mr. Hunter. The more elevated tastes." He sighed. "I'm afraid you wouldn't understand."

"Yeah." The detective produced his own crumpled pack, crossed to the end table for a match. The match folder bore the legend, Distinctive Tobacco Products Company. Hunter stared at it for a long moment before lighting up. Finally, he looked away from it to ask, "Well? What about Williams?"

"I know nothing of him."

25

"He knew a lot about you."

"Yes?"

"He knew, for instance, that you're a crook . . . that the —what do you call 'em?—oh yes, the concrete cylinders you tested on the Belt Boulevard were deficient."

"Indeed?" The little man tried to look indignant. He ended up stamping his foot. "He was wrong."

"Forty years a chemist and he was wrong?"

"Mr. Hunter," the baby-face man's tone dripped sarcasm, "if you suspect that my tests of materials on the Belt Boulevard were inaccurate, why don't you take your complaint to the engineers who supervised the construction for the city?"

"And they would be?"

"They would be—" he paused dramatically "—the firm of Kennedy and Blake!"

Hunter's hands tightened convulsively. His eyes froze. But the thin face remained impassive. He thought a moment, then said, "Maybe I will." Fury blazed in his eyes. He took a half-step forward. "But I'll be back. Never fear— I'll be back."

The little man cringed.

Hunter smiled contemptuously, then left.

Except for the operator, the elevator that came to take him down from Westrope's was empty. Peter Hunter waited until the doors had slid shut. Then his deft hand darted out, removed the hand that held the car's controls.

The elevator operator, a boy of seventeen, turned. "Floor, sir?" he asked.

Hunter waved a dollar bill. "This is for your dear old mother, home praying you meet no temptation in this voluptuous temple of sin."

26

"Nuts to that," the boy snapped. "The old lady's out at the track." He snatched at the bill.

"Not so fast. I'm buying information."

"Sure thing. There's one on the third floor. I'll okay you with the madam and you won't have no trouble. Nice, refined joint."

Hunter shook his head sadly. The boy said, "Snap it up, buddy. The starter's signalling me to take 'er down."

"The man in eight fourteen is going to make some telephone calls in a minute or so. I'd like you to get the numbers he calls from the switchboard downstairs."

The boy looked at the dollar. "It ain't worth it."

"For how much?"

"Five."

Hunter nodded. "It's a deal."

The car shot down as if jet-propelled. Hunter went into the lobby and found a seat near a potted palm. The boy was back in five minutes. He took the five dollar bill and handed Hunter two slips of paper.

Hunter patted his head. "Nice work, Horatio. You may never marry the boss's daughter. But—if she has any illegitimate children, I'll lay even money they're yours."

The boy accepted the accolade modestly.

Hunter watched him go back to the car, then turned his eyes down to the two slips.

One was a number he didn't know. When he looked it up, it turned out to be that of Mike Wyatt.

The second he knew very well.

It belonged to George Kennedy!

He drove back to the offices of Kennedy and Blake. There, the receptionist in the waiting room, at mention of his name,

27

referred him immediately to George Kennedy's private offices.

He came into the inner office so quietly that the girl at the desk wasn't aware of an alien presence until she heard the click of the closing door.

Hunter smiled at her, and his taut face seemed to relax. The hard mouth softened and the frozen eyes gained warmth. The smile widened into a crooked grin that was at once both mischievous and charming.

"You're Peg Wyatt," he said.

The girl nodded.

His glance admired her frankly—the small heart-shaped face, the full parted lips. Her eyes were deep blue. They seemed to be bottomless. Her small white teeth were a perfect semi-circle of gleaming pearly-white.

"You look pretty that way—with the surprise in your eyes," he said approvingly.

She didn't color, nor did his inspection cause her any embarrassment. She met his admiration with a faint, self-possessed lift of the eyebrows. After a moment, she smiled back at him gravely.

"Your boss in?"

Her eyes measured him before she said, "No." She consulted her desk calendar. "He's addressing a hospital dedication." Her voice was low in pitch, yet remarkably clear. It had a strange luminous quality. "After that, there's a luncheon. He won't be back for several hours."

Hunter snapped his fingers impatiently. He seemed to waver between leaving immediately and staying to talk.

She said, "Can I help you?"

His eyes studied her. "It all depends," he said slowly. "How much do you know about what I'm supposed to be doing for your boss?"

She weighed her words before answering. "I know you

28

were engaged to find Samuel Williams. That's all I know."

"It's enough." He pulled a wooden office chair up to her desk and sat down. "What kind of guy was Samuel Williams?"

She smiled faintly, like a little girl with a secret joke. "Did you ever see his picture?"

Hunter nodded.

"He was just like his picture."

"Then he didn't run away—he's really missing."

Again, she considered her words carefully before saying, "I think so." There was the faint enigmatic smile before she asked, "Anything else?"

"Even if there wasn't, I'd think of something."

"Oh?"

"Just to stay here."

She accepted the compliment with a nod. But genuine pleasure lighted her deep blue eyes.

He waited for her to talk, but she said nothing. Finally, he said, "How about Westrope—another chemist? Little guy. Know him, too?"

The smile faded. The light in her eyes went out. "I know him," she said. "Yes, I know him."

"He just told me this office would vouch for his integrity," Hunter said. Unwittingly, his voice had sharpened. His hands were taut and groping, his eyes intense. He had resumed his professional guise.

"Mr. Westrope tested materials on the Belt Boulevard project. We were the supervising engineers. So far as I know, there were no complaints about his work."

Her voice had lost the luminous quality. It became flat and uninflected. She averted her eyes. It was as if she had withdrawn her personality from the conversation.

He said, "Oh," in such a way that she jerked her eyes back to his face.

29

"How well did you know him?" Hunter asked.

She didn't answer.

"I gather," he said deliberately, "that *your* dealings with Westrope went beyond the impersonal business phase."

She looked down at her hands. They lay perfectly still in her lap. "Just once," she said, and her voice was a whisper.

"And did you—"

"I'd rather not talk about it." She spoke crisply, but without losing her composure.

Their eyes met. She lifted her head defiantly.

"Okay," he said. He smiled, but the fingers of his right hand remained—strained, dissatisfied. "We'll speak of something else."

"Please do."

"Are you the daughter of Mike Wyatt, the politician?"

"More skeletons." She began to laugh. A clear, merry sound. "No—his niece."

"And what do you do here?"

"I'm Mr. Kennedy's secretary."

"Since when?"

"For the last six months." She laughed again. "I'm beginning to think I can read your mind."

"And it's nasty, isn't it?" He smiled. "When you laugh, it sounds good." He waited a moment, then remarked pleasantly, "I figure your Uncle Mike put you here to keep tabs on his candidate for mayor."

Fer eyes widened in admiration. "You're very clever." Her voice sank to a whisper, but she did not blush. Nor did she betray any embarrassment.

Her praise pleased him. "It's my business," he explained.

The phone buzzed. She picked it up. She said, "No, Mr. Kennedy is out . . . Not until late this afternoon . . ."

Hunter leaned forward.

She said, "Yes, I'll remind him," and jotted a phone number on the desk pad. She hesitated momentarily, then said, "Yes, I'll take care of it immediately." She hung up.

To Hunter she said, "Will you excuse me—there's something I must do now." She rose and walked to the door.

His eyes were hard as he followed her. She moved with a sinuous grace. Her body was slim, her breasts small but well-formed. There was something feline about her as she walked—a sense of soft padded symmetry.

He frowned at her back. But, when he spoke, his face smiled. He said, "I can tell you something else, too."

Hand on the knob, she turned on the door. A cryptic half-smile masked her thoughts. "Yes?"

"You have nothing to take care of. That guy hung up right after he gave you his phone number. You just threw in that extra line so you could get away from me."

The small full mouth twitched, but the face remained enigmatic. "That, too," she admitted, "was very clever, Mr. Hunter."

"But," she added, and her voice was luminously clear, "there really isn't anything you can do about it, is there?"

And she walked out.

4

THEY WERE WAITING for him when he came out.

There was a man sitting behind the wheel of Hunter's car. His face was small and pinched. He had dirty gray eyes that scurried around in the bony sockets like flitting mice. He looked up when the slim detective approached.

Hunter opened the car door. "What's the pitch?" he demanded. "Who the hell are you?"

The dirty gray eyes widened. They darted past Hunter.

Something steely and unyielding bored into the slim detective's back. A hoarse voice wheezed, "Inside, Jack!"

Hunter turned his head six inches. He saw a round battered face with squashed features.

The eyes were empty. Absolutely empty. Vacant. Devoid of meaning.

"And if I don't?"

The empty eyes darkened. The face tensed.

The man behind the wheel yelled, "Don't, Chuck!"

The face relaxed.

The man with the dirty gray eyes said to Hunter, "Don't be a hero, Jack."

Hunter said, "He really would have burned me, wouldn't he?"

"He don't know no better, Jack."

Hunter bounced the ignition key in his hand, then threw it to the sidewalk twenty feet away. His eyes blazed as he snarled, "All right, there it is. What do you do now? Drill me, run over, pick up the key and make a getaway?" His voice became a sneer and he actually snapped his fingers in the face of the empty-eyed killer behind him. "You punks with the big-talk give me a pain. Trying to push people around."

"Do I burn him, Muggsy?" The empty-eyed killer was asking for instructions from the man in the car.

Muggsy said, "Not yet, Chuck." He spoke coaxingly to Hunter. "Look, Jack, what're ya makin' all the fuss about? The boss just wants to talk to ya."

"I don't like his invitations."

"Lemme burn 'im, Muggsy."

It was a man's voice but it sounded like a child whining for a piece of cake. It was a strange sound to come wheezing up through the battered larynx of a punchdrunk ex-pug.

"The boss said no, Chuck. The boss said he wants to talk to 'im."

"Just once, Muggsy." Again the whine. "In the belly."

"Who's the boss?" Hunter demanded. "Maybe I don't want to see him."

"Don't make no trouble, Jack. Come quiet and save yourself lumps. The boss owns this town. He wantsa see ya—he'll see ya. If it ain't today, it'll be tomorrer."

Hunter's grin was twisted, garish. "Why didn't Mike Wyatt call me himself?" His angular fingers dismissed the battered killer behind him with a contemptuous gesture. "Pick up the key," he snapped. "Let's get going."

Chuck handed the key to Muggsy. "Just once," he

34

pleaded. "In the belly." There was hate in the once-empty eyes.

Mike Wyatt measured the detective like a trader estimating the value of the chemicals in his body at a bankruptcy sale. Mike's eyes were yellow-green. Looking into them was like peering into a slum alleyway. Like staring through a milky fog to watch two cats scavenging for hashhouse leftovers.

Mike said: "So *you're* Peter Hunter."

You could hear the conceit in his voice. It covered the man like a coat of slimy armor.

Hunter replied—in exactly the same tone: "So *you're* Mike Wyatt."

Wyatt tried to smile. The yellow-green eyes gleamed. The corners of his mouth twisted upward.

But the expression ended there at the mouth.

Because the facial nerves were paralyzed. The lips quirked, but the face remained as of wood. And the effect was one of supreme frustration.

As though the man was fighting within himself. A furious struggle that might destroy the onlooker.

Again, Mike tried to smile. "You'll remember me."

"Yes?"

"A long long time." The voice was scornful. It was a goad, with the man's ego as its gleaming point.

Hunter's voice snapped like a whip. "I'll remember you—long after you're dead!"

Chuck's fist cracked out, cuffed him savagely on the side of the head.

Hunter whirled.

The gun lifted. The battered face snarled. The vacant eyes were two slits.

Hunter drew a deep breath. He forced his hands down to his sides.

The clutching fingers twitched savagely.

"I wanted to smoke 'im, boss." The wheezing voice whined. "Muggsy stopped me."

"What a pity, Chuck." The smile the politician's face couldn't form seemed to hang aborted in the air.

Hunter choked on his pent-up fury. "I'll pay that back," he rasped.

"Come, come, Hunter," Wyatt chided blandly. "Don't be hard on Chuck. He's just impulsive."

The fury blazed higher in Hunter's eyes. The cruel lips sharpened down to a razor edge.

"Chuck is solicitous after my prestige, Hunter. He knows me well. He merely demands that you accept me at his valuation, that you make the proper obeisance." He turned to the empty-eyed killer. "Am I right, Chuck?"

"Muggsy shouldn'ta stopped me."

Wyatt laughed. The sound came through. The face remained frozen in the frustration of its paralysis.

"So you're the king," Hunter sneered. "Making with the polysyllabics to impress a lamebrain, punchdrunk yegg. And he can't even hear the contempt behind the rhetoric."

"Contempt is the wrong word, my friend. Let us say, *superiority*. Chuck hears it and he accepts it.

Hunter laughed harshly. "You're a helluva king if *he's* all you can brag about."

Anger glowed yellow in Wyatt's eyes. Sensing it, Chuck moved forward. "Just once, Boss," he begged. "In the belly."

Wyatt shook his head. "Hunter, I brought you here to warn you. I want you to stop your snooping. Is that clear?"

"No." The word cracked out like a shot. He stuck out his jaw. The live hands balled into fists.

"I own this town, Hunter. I can break you in half. I'm

doing it the easy way—for you. I'm warning you: forget the Williams matter—if you enjoy living."

Hunter stabbed an electric finger at the politician's frozen face. "You're just a cheap crook," he sneered. "Just another punk. And you'll go down—just like the rest."

At the word *punk*, Wyatt's eyebrows scissored angrily. He bit hard into his lip. The yellow eyes glowed.

But, through the storm, the face remained like stone. Eerily unmoved.

Hunter plodded on. "You're no different. You talk better but you think just as dirty. You're educated—you'll wind up in the prison library."

It should have been ridiculous: A lone slim man with a crooked nose and a twisted face defying a politician who had an entire city under his thumb and owned his own police force.

But it roused Mike Wyatt to a terrible anger.

He jerked his head at Chuck. The empty-faced killer slammed the gun hard against the side of Hunter's head.

Hunter fell to his knees. Savagely, Chuck torpedoed the point of his shoe against the detective's ribs. The breath soughed out of Hunter's lungs in a groan.

Through the red mist that fogged his glazed eyes Hunter stared malevolently into the face of the killer.

Chuck's hand tightened on the gun. His eyes burned. They flamed with an ecstatic passion.

Hunter fought the clammy fist of nausea at his stomach. His own voice was a booming echo in his whirling head . . . the sound of a hammer beating out words on an empty boiler.

But his lips pulled back in a garish snarl that bared his sharp, rending teeth. And the defiant words came gritting out. "Wyatt, you cheap punk—what happens when you let him pull the trigger?"

37

Then the gun barrel sledged full on his bare skull. The flares exploded in his head. The noise swelled to the volume of a barrage. He pitched forward on his face.

He heard the door open. As though it came winding down a long tunnel, he heard Muggsy's voice, eerily remote, say, "Kennedy's downstairs, boss. Says he has an appointment."

Then he heard no more.

For a moment after the slim body folded, the hands continued to twitch. As though they had not surrendered. As though they still fought to retain the last residual spark of consciousness.

Then it was over. The gallant hands, too, lay motionless.

Mike Wyatt stood over him trembling. The breath panted out of his distended nostrils. A hurricane of hate stormed in the yellow eyes.

And, through it all, the face stayed strangely still as stone.

He glared down at the unconscious form. He kicked the motionless body.

"Lay it in a ditch somewhere," he snarled.

Peter Hunter regained consciousness all at once. There were no questions about where he was or what had happened. One minute, he was out: the next, he had opened his eyes. His fingers tensed. It was as if he had never been unconscious.

He lifted his head. The movement gouged an expression of pain into his face. But his lips remained clamped. No sound escaped them.

His hand went behind his ear. He felt the swelling there He touched his swollen face gingerly.

Then he tried to sit up.

His face went white. He clutched at his ribs. A groan escaped him.

"Take it easy," Tim said soothingly. "What happened?"

"Mike Wyatt." He cursed the politician and his entire organization.

He forced himself into a sitting position. If the attempt caused him pain, his face did not reveal it.

He said, "What time is it?"

"About three."

"Still Thursday?"

"Yes."

"How did I get home?"

"Some kids found you under a tree near Crotona Avenue. They got an ambulance. You had a helluva battle with the interne, made him bring you here instead of to the hospital."

Hunter frowned. "Funny. Can't remember any of it."

He swung his legs over the side of the bed. His feet touched the floor. He swayed, seemed about to faint.

Tim reached out to steady him. Hunter knocked the hand away, gripped the surface of the night table savagely. After a moment, he sighed. Deeply.

He took a few shaky steps.

Moloney said, in a tone that accepted defeat before the battle. "Doc wants you to stay in bed."

Hunter snorted. He tottered into the living room. From the liquor cabinet, he took a squat bottle and poured two stiff drinks. He handed one to Tim and downed his own in one swallow. He poured himself another.

"What the hell did you find out today?" Hunter asked. He lowered himself onto the couch.

"You'll probably drop dead any minute. You certainly don't deserve any better."

Hunter smiled indulgently. "Okay, you've done your duty. Now let's have the dope."

39

The skinny man sighed hopelessly. "You want to know about the Belt Boulevard?"

"I want to know about everything."

Tim leaned forward. "It cost over five million. It was built to route through traffic around the outskirts of the city, thereby reducing downtown congestion."

"Where does Kennedy come in?"

"Like this: For a project this big, the city fathers felt that the mediocrities on their civil service staff would be out of their engineering depth. So, an outside firm was engaged to design the project and supervise its construction. Enter Kennedy and Blake."

"When was this?"

"1946." Moloney paused significantly. "Kennedy was still in the army. Helping the Burmese government on construction problems. Didn't get back until '47."

"Why were Kennedy and Blake hired?"

"Because of the firm's recognized genius. And," Tim rolled his eyes wickedly, "because of its connections."

"Okay. Go on."

"Despite your suspicious mind, the firm is supposed to have done an outstanding job. Cloverleafs, underpasses, bypasses, overpasses—I won't bother your aching head with the finer details."

"But Kennedy had nothing to do with it?"

"He had drawn the plans before the war, but the outbreak of hostilities ended all public construction. After the war, when the work was done, the entire production was under the direct personal supervision of Mr. James Blake, the junior partner of the firm. And—right now, no one knows where *he* is."

"I know."

"Where?"

40

"Flew into Canada last week to go hunting. That's what Kennedy told me."

"Oh."

Quite suddenly, Hunter put his hand to his bandaged ribs. His eyes closed. His free hand tightened into a fist.

"Pete!" Moloney jumped up, ran to him.

Hunter opened his eyes. Breath whistled out through his nostrils.

"For God's sake, Pete—"

Hunter stared at him. "What'd you find out about Williams?" he demanded harshly.

"But your ribs, man—"

Hunter put his hand on his partner's arm. "It's all right, Timmy," he said, gently. "But don't you see," a steely note came into his voice, "this case is the only way I can get back at Wyatt?"

Tim met the stare of the frozen blue eyes. "You're mad," he said. "Stark, staring mad. But—I'll tell you about Williams."

"Good."

"I used those pictures. One of the bus drivers recognized him. Monday night, about seven forty, he took a B-23 bus one block from his home and rode to the corner of Crescent and Water Streets."

Hunter's hands stiffened. He leaned forward.

"At about eight fifteen," Tim said, "he went into a saloon called Spero's."

"Williams—in one of those dirty little gin mills down there?"

"Improbable as it sounds—yes. In ten minutes, he was joined by a gentleman who, according to the description I got, could have been none other than our client, George Kennedy."

41

The hands jumped. "You're sure?"

"Certain."

"How long did they stay?"

"About fifteen minutes. The bartender suggests they might have been arguing."

"They went out together?"

"Together."

"What happened to Williams then?"

"No one knows. He disappeared."

"The bus drivers?"

"They don't remember him."

"Cabs?"

"I checked. No dice."

"Did he go off with Kennedy?"

Moloney hesitated. "He could have."

"You don't know for sure?"

"No."

"You'll have to keep looking."

"Okay."

Hunter leaned back. His eyes were remote. Cigarette smoke feathered out of his nostrils and through the thin lips. The telltale hands moved, in the characteristic gesture of rubbing against each other . . . Examining the fabric of the facts.

Tim said: "One more thing."

Hunter turned to him. "Shoot."

"A lot of rumors about the election. They say Kennedy is going to appoint Ed Montgomery to be chairman of the new Housing Authority."

"Montgomery." Hunter scowled. "That conscienceless bastard."

"Exactly."

Hunter looked down at his hands. "Before I'm through—"

42

The phone rang. Hunter's quick hand snaked out, lifted it off its cradle. "Hello . . . Speaking."

The voice at the other end was excited. Hunter's muscles bunched as he listened. The vibrant hands tightened. "Sit tight," he snapped. "I'm on my way." He hung up.

He turned abruptly. "Kennedy." The excitement smoldered in his eyes. "At Westrope's hotel. Sounds as if the world fell on his head."

"You big jerk," Moloney stormed, "you can't go out."

Hunter's grin was electric. "Oh, can't I!"

5

PETER HUNTER passed through the lobby of West-rope's apartment hotel quickly and unostentatiously. At the entrance to the bar, he paused. His eyes swept its interior like the muzzle of a machine gun.

George Kennedy was sitting in a booth. Hunter crossed to him quickly. "What gives?"

The engineer frowned so hard that the wrinkles left ugly red creases on his smooth brow. He breathed deeply and closed his eyes. When he opened them again, his manner had regained its usual easy decisiveness.

"A chemist named Westrope called me. My secretary got the call about one thirty. While I was out to lunch."

"One thirty!" Hunter looked at his watch. "Three hours ago!"

"I didn't get back to the office until three." He hesitated. "Something came up. A conference."

"When'd you get here?"

"About three forty-five. I went right up."

"Yes?"

"He's dead."

"How?"

"Shot."

"I'm not surprised. He knew too much. You called the police?"

"No. I thought you'd want to see for yourself."

"Good." Hunter stood. A sudden thought struck him. "If he was dead, how'd you get in?"

Kennedy's eyebrows arched. "The door was unlocked."

It was still unlocked when they got upstairs. The curtains swayed in the breeze from the open windows. Packed and closed, two suitcases stood beside the glass-fronted bookcase.

"The bedroom," Kennedy said tautly.

A brand new trunk, open and half full gaped beside the bed. Westrope lay slumped against it, face down. The back of his head was a shattered shambles. A fudge of congealing blood lay in a pool on the floor.

"He's very dead," Hunter said softly. He bent to the body. "Powder burns. Small caliber or his head would be even worse. Probably while packing."

Deftly, his hands tilted the corpse to one side, then the other. The lithe fingers probed the pockets. The wallet had some business cards, plane tickets to Havana, about thirty dollars in cash.

"Not kosher," he muttered.

He turned to the trunk. Seven suits hung in the wardrobe half. Two of them were women's; one gray, the other slate blue.

"Not going alone."

They returned to the living room. Hunter slipped a metal tool from his key ring into the lock of each of the suitcases. He pressed gently. They opened.

Among some nylon shirts, he found a small pigskin bag

46

the size of a shaving case. It contained two hypodermics, several gleaming steel needles. There were ten glassine envelopes, each filled with a fine-grained powder.

He sniffed. "Heroin."

"A drug addict?" Kennedy was surprised.

Hunter nodded. He knelt beside the second suitcase, found nothing worthy of note. He repacked both suitcases just as he had found them.

He stood. "Let's get the law up here?"

Kennedy met his eyes. "Must we?"

"This is murder."

"Must we both stay?"

"Yes, They'll nose around, find twenty people who saw us in the bar, together. So, we'll call the cops together. Tell them just what happened. Westrope called you . . . he wanted to see you . . . you don't know why. You called me . . . we came . . . found this . . . called them. That's all. No trimmings."

Kennedy nodded. "Whatever you say."

"Don't worry," Hunter said with faint irony. "Wyatt still owns the D.A. He'll protect your political chestnuts."

He picked up the phone, gave the switchboard the district attorney's number. While waiting, he shook a cigarette out of the pack on the table. The perfume from it made him wrinkle his nose in disgust.

The connection went through. Carefully, he reported that Westrope lay dead in room eight fourteen of the hotel, then hung up.

He decided to smoke the cigarette after all, examined the matchbook curiously, lighted one, put the packet in his pocket.

"Careful," Kennedy suggested, half in jest. "It might be drugged."

Hunter dragged deeply. "I never dreamed," he said point-

47

edly, "that a nice well-bred lad like you would jest in the face of death."

Kennedy's face sobered. "It's not the death that bothers me," he said seriously. "I saw enough of that during the war to be able to accept it. It's when you find it, ugly and violent, in the quiet city you grew up in. All through the war I looked back to this as the place where death was peaceful, natural. And now this . . ." His voice trailed off.

Hunter said: "Stop—you'll have me in tears."

The police arrived at five-fifteen. There was organized chaos while the various technicians began their individual specialties. Fingerprint men . . . ballistics . . . photographers . . . all the others as well, in a mad welter of sound and scurrying.

At five-forty, a huge inspector named Kevin Grogan shoved his mountainous bulk into the apartment. He had a solid boulder of a head set into ledge-like shoulders without benefit of neck. Almost imperceptibly, under his direction, the chaos was synchronized . . . the massive vehicle of police procedure began to travel down a well-worn trail.

The Medical Examiner arrived at six. Grogan ushered him into the bedroom to examine the corpse. He came hurrying out five minutes later.

"Death by gunshot, it looks like," he announced. "Close range. Contact, probably. Six to eight hours. Tell you more later." He rushed out.

Grogan came over to where Hunter and Kennedy were standing. "You found him?" he asked.

His voice came out of the big round chest, deep and rumbling. He spoke slowly, waited patiently for his answer. Like the mountain he resembled, he seemed to have all the time in the world.

48

Kennedy said, "He asked me to come up to see him. He was dead when we arrived."

A detective came in from outside with some slips in his hand, gave them to Grogan. "He made four calls, Inspector. This one—" he pointed to one of the slips— "to the bank, the other to the airport."

"What about these two?"

The detective bent close to Grogan, whispered in his ear. Grogan nodded, turned searching granite-colored eyes at Kennedy.

"What did he want with you?" he asked Kennedy.

"I don't know."

The room emptied out quickly. Each of the experts, as he left, reported spot impressions to the mountainous Grogan. He listened, apathetically, nodding from time to time. Finally, only Grogan, Hunter, Kennedy and a stenographer remained.

Kevin Grogan deposited his vast bulk in one of the spindly gilt chairs. The cigarette looked like a wisp of straw in his huge, full-moon face. He took it out of his mouth. It seemed lost in his hamlike paw.

"Now," he said deliberately to Kennedy, "tell me again— real slow—how you happened to come up here and find him."

Kennedy repeated the story he and Hunter had agreed on. Grogan listened with patient care, the boulder-like head cocked to a side as though to catch every nuance. Finally, he said, "The same story you told me before. Word for word the same."

"He's talking about the same thing," Hunter snapped. "You want him to color it for your entertainment."

The huge head swiveled slowly to Hunter. "You're corroborating this story?"

49

"As far as I can. But what the hell—you got men checking it. You'll soon know how kosher it is."

"You're working for Mr. Kennedy?"

"I work for myself."

Grogan shifted his weight ponderously. "He's your client?"

Kennedy broke in to say, "Yes, Inspector—Mr. Hunter is working for me on a personal matter."

"Might I know the nature of it?"

"You heard the nature of it," Hunter snapped. "It's personal. The word, 'personal,' is not an invitation for a nosy cop to butt in."

Imperturbably, Grogan asked, "Did it concern Westrope?"

"It was personal. Period."

The big man turned back to Kennedy. "You had no idea what Westrope wanted?"

"You heard him," Hunter cut in. "None."

"Odd." The word came out in a deep sigh.

"Odd!" Hunter exclaimed. "Odd! That cookie wasn't anything but odd. See those books? Those pictures? He was a real gypsy."

Kennedy stood. "Inspector, I really must be going. I'm scheduled to address a veterans' meeting tonight."

"Of course. You'll hold yourself available?"

"Certainly." Kennedy left.

Grogan watched him out the door, then said, "I've been meaning to have a word with you, Hunter."

"Honest, Mr. Policeman, I'm innocent."

Grogan's head revolved slowly so that he could survey the whole room. It was a movement as ponderous as the revolution of a gun turret on a Sherman tank.

"I hear you've been looking into this Williams business," he said finally. "Where do you fit into it?"

"You want to talk to me?" Hunter asked meaningfully.

50

"I'm trying to."

"Then ditch the writing machine." He jerked his head at the stenographer.

"You got something to hide?"

"I'm shy. I don't want to talk for publication."

Hotly, the stenographer said, "You can rely on—"

"I know, sonny," Hunter cut in. "Your discretion is impeccable. Absolutely impeccable. But I'm sensitive. I don't like the things I say published by anyone. Not even by people with absolutely impeccable discretion."

"All right, Hughes," Grogan conceded gently. "I'll talk to Mr. Hunter alone."

The stenographer snatched up his pad and pencil angrily. He left, glaring over his shoulder at Hunter.

"You could have relied on him," Grogan said.

"Yeah. I could've relied on him. I could've relied on him to make a fine memorandum of whatever I said. I could've relied on him to turn a copy of that memo over to Mike Wyatt as soon as he left. That's what I could've relied on him for."

"And why would Wyatt be so interested in you?"

"You tell me." His hands touched the bandage on his ribs. "Tell me why he had his gunsel pistol-whip me this morning. Why he wants me to lay off this Williams business."

"You *are* hot about this Williams, aren't you?"

"How do *you* feel about it?"

"We're not discussing me."

Hunter clenched a bony fist. "No, and we're not going to sit here discussing me, either."

Grogan lifted his eyes to the ceiling. "Why do I always get the stubborn ones?" he complained. He leaned forward. "This is the second killing we've had today."

"Should I know about the other?"

51

"You might. It came about noon. A guy named Malbin."

Hunter's eyes gleamed. "I suppose he was in the construction business too."

Grogan whistled softly. "You guessing? Or do you know?"

"That's your guess now."

The phone rang. Grogan hoisted himself over to it. He listened, then asked, "That all?" nodded and hung up.

"One of my men. Located Westrope's secretary. She tells of a guy named Hunter who was anxious to see her boss."

"I did see him. Today."

"Why?"

Hunter looked down at his stiff hands. He jammed them into his pockets. He shook his head doggedly.

"I'm giving you every break I can, boy," Grogan reminded him softly. "But, you know it can't go on this way."

Hunter clamped his lips shut.

"Are all you private snoopers the offspring of mules? Are you really this dumb? Or do you want the law to break down so you can make more dough?"

"Dumb!" The word seemed to touch a raw spot. "Do *I* want the law to break down?" Hunter's voice grated. "You got a right to ask, haven't you? An old chemist is snatched. What'd you come up with? Nothing. This gypsy lover gets his head knocked off—and you badger *me*. You know goddam well I had nothing to do with it. Malbin gets fogged. Are you out dogging the killer? Hell no, you're sitting with me—playing the heavy cop."

Grogan slapped his huge paw against his thigh. "So what?"

"So this: I, for one, wonder whether you're trying to find a killer—or trying to *cover* for one?"

In Grogan's temple, a vein began to pump like an agitated heart. The fight for self-control showed in his clenched jaw. "That is stiff talk," he said with tense softness. "It deserves a chaser."

52

Baleful and blue-white, Hunter's eyes glittered. His hands leaped out of his pockets to gesture angularly.

"Sure," he rasped, "but I doubt if you'll take it."

"Try me."

"Okay—what're you doing about Samuel Williams?"

Grogan appeared to flinch. "They pulled me off it," he said lamely.

"Yeah, Mike Wyatt owns the D.A. and Mayor Burkett owns the cops. The D.A. won't embarrass Mike. The cops won't upset Burkett." He reached into his pocket, threw Grogan the packet of matches he had found earlier on the telephone table. "Read that: 'Distinctive Tobacco Products, Inc.' You saw the hypo this gypsy had. Will you check on Distinctive Tobacco Products, the place he got his snow? Did you follow up when you learned Williams was in Spero's the night he was snatched? So what? So nothing. You do what you get paid for. Okay—but let me *earn* my dough."

Grogan turned his eyes down to the floor. He slumped in the chair.

The slim detective's tone softened. "Don't take it personally. I know you'd be chief of police if there was any honesty in this town's government. I know you got a family and kids have healthy appetites. But I also know you're going to avoid all the rackets so the kids can keep eating."

Grogan spread huge palms. "What can I do?"

"I don't know. Wait until *Distinctive* has a distinctive pack of reefers in the pocket of every kid in town, I guess."

"Come now—it's not that bad."

"Not yet, it isn't, you mean."

"It never will be."

"Not 'cause they're afraid of you. They're just smart enough not to louse up a fat racket by overworking it."

"But what can *I* do?"

53

"Do! Don't hound the guy who's trying to clean the mess up."

"Meaning you?"

"Who else?" He paused, added, "And you know *I'm* clean."

Grogan clenched a massive fist. "You think I'd take this talk from a punk?"

Hunter grinned.

Grogan opened the fist. The big round face showed concern. "You don't stand a chance if you lose. Wyatt'll never forget."

Hunter's eyes were suddenly remote. "I know it."

Grogan got to his feet. "I don't have your faith, boy. But, goddammit, I won't stand in your way. Get the hell out of here."

Hunter's grin was mischievous. "You'll brag about this to your kids some day."

"Get out—and good luck to you."

6

IT WAS six thirty when Peter Hunter left Grogan in the apartment of the late Westrope. An hour later, after a quick dinner, he parked his car in front of the Barclay mansion. He went up the wide steps slowly, stood on the columned porch for a moment, looking around, before he rang the bell.

An aged butler answered. Instead of admitting Hunter, the old man came out and closed the door behind him. His eyes were tired and bloodshot. It looked as if he'd gone without sleep for a long time.

Hunter apologized for the intrusion on their mourning. His business was urgent. He would like to see Miss Barclay.

The old man's tired eyes narrowed apprehensively. He shook his head and barred entrance to the house with his frail body.

What, he wanted to know, was the nature of Mr. Hunter's business with Miss Barclay?

A confidential matter.

He was told, firmly, that Miss Barclay was not available.

"It's about her father's suicide," Hunter said.

55

"Yes?"

"I've seen the audit of the estate. There isn't a penny left."

"Miss Myra is independently wealthy," the butler said. It was as if he was trying to defend the dead man.

"Listen," Hunter said with soft insistence. "Barclay was forced into suicide. He was being blackmailed. He killed himself to escape."

The butler waited for more.

"I'm after the same people who caused his death. With your help—and Miss Barclay's—I may be able to clear his name."

The old man eyed him shrewdly. "With all due respect, sir, how do I know you're a friend?"

"Simply because I'm here. I could have gone to the police."

The tired old eyes went to the crepe on the door, seeking guidance there. His shoulders sagged. "Maybe I shouldn't . . . I need help, sir."

"I'll do what I can."

"And you will tell no one?"

Hunter promised fervently.

The butler opened the door. Hunter stepped inside, heard the distant keening of slow blues music.

The butler's face was abject. "I just can't stop her, sir."

"How long has this been going on?"

"Since Mr. Barclay . . ."

"Where is she?"

The old man led him to a closed door off the foyer. When he opened it, the music flared up, mournful and slow.

Myra Barclay, ghastly sallow, turned muddy eyes at them, made unavailing efforts to rise from a green velvet chair. Hunter bent to look into her face.

"Hopped to the ears."

56

His eyes shifted to the endtable beside the chair. There were several crumpled packs of cigarettes, an ashtray full of butts and two books of matches. Hunter picked up one of the matchbooks. His jaw jutted angrily.

The measured melancholy of the music ran to its mournful end. Machinery clicked as another record dropped to the turntable. A sax began its long lugubrious bleat.

Hunter hurried to the machine, switched it off. The bleat became a groan as the record slowed, stopped.

Myra Barclay swayed to her feet, tottered toward the record player. Hunter shook his head at the butler. The old man moved to intercept her.

He put his arms around her. She clung to him. He led her back to the chair.

Hunter squatted before her. The foulness of her breath, typical of drug addiction, made him turn his head for a moment.

He said, "Myra, I want to talk to you."

Her head lolled. Her eyes remained closed.

"About your father."

The muddy eyes opened. "I killed him," she said.

"You took a gun and shot him?"

"No."

"Then how?"

She closed her eyes.

"Tell me. I can help you."

"No help." She began to cry. Mewling sobs. Like an animal. "Go 'way. Lea' me 'lone. I killed him."

Hunter stared at her. Her head fell forward to her chest. Hunter straightened, signalled the butler to follow him outside.

In the foyer, he asked, "How long has this been going on?"

"Two years." He paused, then said, "It's not her fault.

57

She was in an auto accident, suffered terribly. They gave her drugs. She wasn't strong enough to resist."

"Mr. Barclay knew about this?"

The old man nodded.

"And he didn't get a doctor?"

"He wanted to keep it a secret. At first, he tried to with-hold the . . . whatever it is she needs. That almost drove her mad. After that, he merely looked after her."

Hunter shook his head in irritation.

"If you please, sir, about this business of having killed him—why does she keep saying that? She couldn't have: she was downstairs . . . when it happened."

"A guilt complex. Better get a doctor quick. Before she attempts suicide."

"Suicide!"

"Better hurry. Right now."

The old man turned to the telephone table, remembered something and turned back to Hunter. "I'm relying on your silence," he reminded the detective.

"Like the grave."

He went out while the old man was still waiting for the connection. As he walked toward the car, he looked down at the matchfolder, still clutched in his hand.

His thin lips writhed angrily as he tore it to shreds.

At eight twenty-five that same evening, Peter Hunter stood before the door of Peg Wyatt's apartment, holding a bouquet of cornflowers. For a moment, he looked down at his clothes, flicked an imaginary speck of lint off his lapel. He drew a deep breath and pressed the button.

She opened the door. A smile of genuine pleasure lighted her face when she saw him. Her deep blue eyes brightened. She looked very lovely and, somehow, quite girlish.

Hunter grinned. "I was passing by. Thought I'd stop in."

Her lips toyed with the faintest of skeptical smiles. A guarded look came into her eyes. "Just an impulse?" Her tongue puffed her cheek.

"You could call it that." He offered the cornflowers. "They reminded me of your eyes."

"How did you know where I lived? And how—"

He laid a quick finger to her lips. "Don't ask questions." He made a comic-opera gesture, hand to his heart. "Let's not let cynicism destroy something that might turn out very beautiful."

She smiled again, then led the way inside. "They *are* lovely," she said, and pressed her face into the flowers. Her eyes had a sheen to them. "Thank you."

She was wearing a blue quilted satin robe over pink pajamas. Her soft blonde hair was cut short and curled naturally. She looked like a little girl about to go to bed.

"No lovelier than you," he said, sincerely.

She didn't blush. She acknowledged the compliment with a slight nod. As if it was no more than her due.

"I like your poise, too, kitten," he said. "It's nice to see a woman accept the nice things people say as if they belong to her. Without blushing. Without giggling."

She smiled faintly.

"And I like your place." He stood in the center of the room and looked around. "I like it a lot."

It was restful, a soft blend of old rose and deep blues with, here and there in the drapes and upholstery fabrics, a feathering of yellow. He turned to her. "It becomes you, kitten."

She had been arranging the flowers in a squat vase on an endtable. But now something in his voice made her look up. His eyes met hers, fastened onto them intently. A soft lovely blush rose to her cheeks.

"I . . ." The deep breath she was forced to take lifted

59

her small but perfectly formed breasts. "I'm glad . . . you like it." She spoke the words almost breathlessly, but her voice had a clear luminousness.

The room was momentarily so silent that the whirring of an electric clock was clearly audible.

Finally, like a man breaking a spell, Hunter cleared his throat. The sound came out harsh and racking.

She turned back to the flowers. He looked at his hands which were for the moment, oddly enough, perfectly still. When he looked at her again, she had opened a cabinet and was holding out a bottle to him.

"Drink?" she asked.

He looked at the label. It was a good Scotch. "With water." While she was in the kitchenette fixing the drinks, he looked into the cabinet. "Wow, kitten—that's quite a cellarful." He winked at her as she returned. "I never took you for the secret-lush type."

"Uncle Mike gave them to me." She waved her hand all-inclusively. "He paid for the whole place. I picked the things out and he paid for them. Down to the last ashtray."

He shook his head dubiously. Obviously, it didn't fit his conception of Mike Wyatt.

"It was his way of getting rid of me," she explained. "After he furnished the place, he bought me a gun and showed me how to use it. I was on my own, he told me."

"Nice feller."

He took his drink and went to a chair. There were books on the endtable beside it. He looked at them curiously. He frowned. "You *read* these, kitten?" There was wonder in his voice.

She sipped at her drink, but made no answer.

He read the titles aloud. " 'Give Your Heart To The

60

Hawks.' 'Be Angry At The Sun.' " He looked at her. "You *like* Jeffers?"

"What's wrong with poetry?"

"Not a thing. But *Jeffers!* To give him the place of honor here. That 'Man is corrupt' stuff. 'Man is disgusting. Man is vicious. Man is rotten. Man is decadent.' You go for *that?*"

"And 'Death is the great gift,' " she finished.

"Really," he said. He took a deep breath. "Really!"

She said nothing. She seemed to be enjoying his discomfiture.

He said, "You probably think someone did Westrope a great favor by knocking him off, don't you?"

"Let's change the subject," she countered. "What brings you here tonight?"

He grinned. "But really—I happened to be passing—"

"Really?" Her wonderful eyes mocked him.

"Really. So I thought I'd—"

"Come, come, Mr. Hunter—we understand each other, you and I. What is it you want to know?" Her voice was pleasantly chiding. She seemed to have perfect self-confidence.

"All right," he said. "Let's pretend I came on business."

"Let's pretend—yes."

"I'm trying to find who killed Westrope."

Her face didn't change expression. "And?"

"I think you can help me."

"How?"

"He called your office today?"

"Yes."

"You're sure it was he? You couldn't have been mistaken?"

"It was he. I know his voice—or knew it."

He leaned forward. His hands were stiff, questing. "*You*

61

got the call personally? You and no one else? You and not George Kennedy, for example?"

"*I* got it."

"What did he say?"

"He wanted Mr. Kennedy to call on him at his apartment. As soon as possible. He sounded quite agitated."

He leaned back to collect his thoughts. The eloquent fingers remained outspread, searching.

"You told Kennedy that when he came back?"

"Yes. It was about three."

"Is it possible that he'd already gotten the message? That Westrope reached him some other way?"

"It's possible—but I doubt it."

"Why?"

She smiled. "Mr. Kennedy's not a very good liar."

"No," he admitted, "he isn't." He said, "Where was Kennedy when you got the phone call from Westrope?"

"I . . ." She hesitated, paused.

"Don't hold out on me, kitten. This is murder."

She ignored his reminder. Her smooth brow furrowed as she followed her own line of thought. Finally she said, "I suppose you'll know soon enough, anyway. He was in conference with my uncle."

"Mike Wyatt."

"Yes." She hesitated again.

"There's more, kitten?"

"You might as well know it all. They quarreled bitterly, he and Uncle Mike. So bitterly that Uncle Mike took the first plane out of town."

"Where to?"

"To the state capitol. To discuss the matter with the governor."

His eyes narrowed. "To discuss *what* matter with the governor?"

62

"Uncle Mike wants George to announce that he's going to appoint Ed Montgomery chairman of the Housing Commission."

"And Kennedy?"

"Refused."

"Refused what? To make the announcement?"

"To make the appointment."

"And Wyatt flew out of town tonight?"

"On the six o'clock plane."

"How do you know?"

"He called the office while Mr. Kennedy was out. He left a message: If George changed his mind, he had until six to let Uncle Mike know."

Hunter looked down at his hands. The slim willowy fingers shifted restlessly. He looked up at her face sharply.

"I was just thinking," he said.

"Yes?"

"If you wanted me to lay off Kennedy. For reasons of your own. Or your uncle's."

"Yes?"

"And you wanted to be smart about it. Real shrewd . . ."

She waited.

"Then you'd probably tell me just what you have. That he knew nothing of the call from Westrope; that he quarreled with Uncle Mike; that he's making like a man and standing on his own two feet."

She stood calmly. Her eyes were steady. Her self-control was almost perfect. The only sign of anger was in her lovely mouth which compressed itself to razor thinness.

She said: "You've finished your drink, Mr. Hunter?"

He looked at the empty glass. "Why, so I have."

"Then I suggest you go. Thank you for the flowers. *They* were lovely."

He got to his feet and faced her. She met his eyes coolly.

63

"Kitten," he said, shaking his head, "I don't begin to understand you. Not one little bit, I don't. And I don't know what you're trying to do." He spoke dispassionately, but his fingers interlaced themselves and tension whitened them at the knuckles.

"But I do know this, kitten. You can't play around in this cesspool without the slime rubbing off on your skirts. You lie to me as if you're covering Kennedy. You can't argue with that—I know it's so. You admit you're in Kennedy's office spying for your uncle. And I know that's so—else how could Uncle Mike know about me so damn quick?"

Her eyes blazed. Her shoulders squared. She threw her head back. Her very posture defied him.

"You're beautiful enough—that I'll admit." He eyed her hungrily. "But—are you cold enough to stand by while someone gets away with murder? To lie in your teeth to protect him?"

He put his hands on her shoulders. She stiffened. But she didn't push him off.

"Well," he asked, and his clenched teeth seemed to warp the rasping words, "how cold are you?"

He stepped toward her. One arm went around her shoulder, the other encircled her waist. She put her hands hard against his arms and fought to push him off. Her struggles seemed to affect him no more than a child's.

He drew her to him. His face went to hers. His lips pressed fiercely on hers. His hand went behind her head, forced it forward. The long slim fingers groped restlessly in her shimmering blonde hair.

She stopped struggling suddenly. Her arms went around his body. Her eyes closed. Her mouth opened. Her body pressed hard against his. Hungrily.

They seemed to melt together. To fuse into one shape.

64

He released her reluctantly. Her face was flushed, her eyes wide, staring. Her nostrils distended as if she was fighting for breath.

She put the back of her hand to her mouth, pressed it hard against her lips. Until the teeth scarred little white marks into her knuckles. It was as if she tried to punish her mouth for having yielded to him.

The robe she wore was half open, the blouse of the pajamas beneath it as well. The nipples of her breasts stabbed hard against the pliant thinness of the pink silk.

He said, breathlessly: "I know, kitten. We both lost control of that one."

He turned and walked out. Without even a backward glance.

Hunter sat in the parked car. The restless excitable fingers were still now, the thin harsh face relaxed. From time to time, he looked out of the car up to the window of Peg Wyatt's apartment. His cold eyes were warm now. Reminiscently, he touched a finger to his lips gently.

He shifted his position on the seat and felt a sharp stab in his ribs where Mike Wyatt's yegg had kicked him. He puffed hard on the cigarette and the winking red light showed his face drawn and gray now.

It was as if, here in the sheltering darkness where pitying eyes could not see, he had allowed the pain to come through . . . he had allowed himself to acknowledge its dominion.

Suddenly, he sat erect. The thin lips began to move wordlessly. His hands stiffened. He threw the car into gear and moved off.

He drove until he came to a drug store, got out and went into a public phone booth. When his connection was es-

65

tablished, he said, "Airport? . . . Give me George Schein in Passenger Service."

He waited impatiently.

"George? . . . Hunter. Peter Hunter. Listen, a guy named Mike Wyatt was booked out on the six o'clock plane to the capitol . . . Yes, the six o'clock plane. . . . Did he actually go? . . . He did? . . . Good. Thanks. 'Bye."

He hung up and made another phone call. "Hello . . . Inspector Grogan, please. . . . Grogan? Hunter. . . . I want to see you right away . . . Yes, right now . . . Any place you say . . . Just so nobody sees us together . . . Where? . . . Front Street off Main? . . . Okay, in five minutes."

Grogan was waiting in the shadow of a building when Hunter drove up. The huge inspector stepped into the car and immediately the younger man had set the vehicle into motion.

Grogan swiveled his massive head and eyed Hunter as he drove. "What's on your mind?" he asked finally.

Hunter turned into a residential street and parked in the darkness provided by a huge elm tree. "What'd you get on Westrope?" he demanded.

Grogan opened a vast empty palm. "Not much. He had reservations on the plane to Havana. For himself and wife. He withdrew ten grand from the bank. He was ducking a guy named Hunter. That's all."

"Where'd he get his dope from?"

Grogan sighed. "Where do they all get it?"

"Distinctive?"

The massive head nodded.

Hunter said, sharply: "Mike Wyatt is out of town."

Grogan frowned. "So what?"

"It's a chance to do something."

Grogan's frown deepened.

66

"Mike's the guy holds the rackets together, you know that. He keeps them covered."

"That's true," the big man admitted quietly.

Hunter turned sharply. "What would happen if a raid was pulled while Mike was away?"

"Now, wait a minute—"

"I'm not asking you to do it. Just listen to me. They'd think Mike had double-crossed them, wouldn't they?"

"They might."

"Okay, here's what I want: Give the word tonight—right away—that there's going to be a dope raid by Homicide. Then—"

"Look, son, if you think I'm going up against Wyatt—"

"I'm not asking you to. Let me finish." The electric fingers gestured excitedly. "Give the word there's going to be a raid. *But*—don't say where. Set the time for—" he looked at his watch "—say, midnight. That'll give me more than two hours."

"And then what?"

"I'll tip the junksters that Mike Wyatt double-crossed them. We'll see what happens."

"What could happen?" Grogan asked dubiously.

"Well, they'd move the stuff out of the store. Someone might—just possibly—try to hijack that stuff in transit."

Grogan's eyes narrowed. "Who?"

Hunter smiled grimly. "I'll take care of that. Now, with Mike away, what would they think?"

"You tell me."

"They might—just possibly—think Mike sold them out."

"They might," Grogan admitted.

"That might upset the status quo around here. That might turn some rocks over. That might give us a clear shot at some of the slimy things hiding under them."

67

"That might," Grogan added quietly, "kiss you into a quick coffin." He hesitated. "I don't like it."

"For God's sake," Hunter yelled, "are you gonna wait till your own kids start pulling on the reefers?"

Grogan said nothing.

"It's my life I'm risking, Grogan. You can cover up. You can raid some other place. Some punk without protection. At worst, you can say someone in your office leaked the info and I tried to pull a fast one. You're clear."

Grogan clenched his hands into boulder-like fists. "Okay, boy, I'll go along with you."

Hunter laughed. "Remember what I told you—you'll brag to your kids some day."

"Yeah. If they don't grow up orphans." He squeezed Hunter's shoulder in his pulverizing grip. "Good luck, boy." He climbed out of the car.

Five minutes later, Hunter had Tim on the phone. "The Distinctive Outfit," he was saying. "Yeah, they'll be loading their dream dust and taking it out of the joint. . . . All you got to do is put a couple of slugs in the tires . . . then go like hell." He grinned. "That's all—make sure you don't miss."

He hung up and his face sobered. For a moment, his fingers probed the burning area of his ribs where he'd been kicked. He winced and a deep sigh forced itself through his tight lips.

Then his face stiffened. He went out to the car.

7

THE TIRES of Peter Hunter's car swished on the gravel
of the huge parking lot as he braked to a stop. Winking
through the darkness, a multi-colored neon rainbow spelled:

ANIMAL FAIR

DINING & DANCING

Hunter switched off the ignition and sat in the car. He
looked at the entrance to the roadhouse as though estimating
the chances of success in his plan. After a moment, he drew
a deep sigh, squared his jaw stubbornly and strode across the
graveled lot.

Once inside, he made his way to the bar, a huge, sculp-
tured-glass-and-neon extravaganza. There were camels
etched in the glass. Amber lights shone from within the
frosted glass, giving it a sun-and-sand garishness. It was
called, appropriately enough, The Oasis.

Hunter ordered Scotch. As he leaned his back against the
bar, drink in hand, the waves of noise rolled toward him,

foaming with raucous laughter. The waiters, costumed in consonance with the decor, wore leopard spotted dinner jackets. But their gait, as they scurried from kitchen to tables, from tables to bar, was most unleopard-like.

Music exploded suddenly, signaling the onset of the floor show. The chorus line legged its way out onto the dime-sized dance floor. Each girl sported a sequin-dotted Juliet cap, out of which sprouted a pair of rhinestone-studded horns. They bobbed their heads and mad glitters of light chased each other around the walls at hysterical speed.

"Quite a show," Hunter said to the bartender.

The bartender's "Yeah," was dubious.

Now, the chorus line turned its back and went into a can-can routine, the maneuver disclosing a short, furry tail extending from each curved, rhinestone posterior. The tails bobbed up and down in unison.

"Now *that*," said Hunter, "is really clever. What genius lost nights of sleep thinking up that?"

The bartender didn't answer.

There was an ad lib laugh as an elderly, white-tied gentleman staggered drunkenly toward one of the chorus pretties, waving a salt shaker and hiccoughing something about "putting salt on its tail to catch it."

A jade with hard white hair and face to match caught him and ultimately succeeded in wrestling him away, explaining all the time that "salt worked only on birds, and these are deers."

Hunter turned back to the bar, caught the bartender's eye. "Who's the lush?"

The bartender eyed him questioningly, as though he knew him and was trying to place him. "Judge Kelland," he answered. "Sits in County Court."

Hunter said, "Quite a judicial figure, isn't he?"

70

The bartender ran a wet finger through the fringe of hair that rimmed his bald, pink skull. "Yeah," he said.

"You've got a ringside seat at quite a circus."

The wet finger began a curl above the bartender's ear. "Useta go to burlesque all the time," he confessed. "Lotsa laughs. But I never go no more."

"Funnier here?"

"Not the show. The audience."

"Whatever happened to the animals you used to keep around the place? The ones in the cages, I mean."

"Couldn't take it. Died."

"Too bad. They used to tone up the place."

The wet finger began another curl. "I think the hyena laughed hisself to death."

"Not at the floor show?"

"No."

Hunter said: "Like all bartenders, you're quite a philosopher."

The bartender leaned forward, the curling finger stopped. "I got a theory."

Hunter smiled. "Elucidate."

"See them tables over there? The ones with tops like turtle shells? Customers get a few shots in 'em, they start yellin' the tables're movin', the turtles is comin' outa their shells." He paused significantly. "But actually—it ain't the *turtles* is comin' outa their shells."

"Very profound, professor."

At this juncture, the judge keeled over at his table. Two waiters hefted him, carried him out. His white-haired companion, following, leered lewdly at Hunter as she passed the bar.

"Demon rum," Hunter said reprovingly.

"That ain't quite fair," the bartender protested.

71

"No?"

"You blame steel 'cause men make bullets out of it?"

"I see your point." Hunter sipped at his drink apprecia-tively. "By the way," he asked, "is Kiki Morrison still around?"

"Yeah." The bartender's wet finger began another curl. "Say, didn't you useta be a friend of hers?"

"We knew the same people." Hunter paid for his drink. "I'd like to see her. You might tell her that Mike Wyatt sent me. The name is Hunter. Peter Hunter."

The bartender stopped the curl. "Sure thing, buddy."

Hunter waited while the bartender telephoned inside. The bartender came back. "She says to go right in, Mr. Hunter."

There was a frozen gleam in the detective's cold blue eyes.

Kiki Morrison lifted her head from the bills she was study-ing. She nodded curtly. She said, "With you in a minute," crisply, made a final notation and stood to exchange a brisk handshake.

Even as she smiled her guarded smile, her eyes measured him. Emerald green they were, shallow, and hard as dia-monds. Her skin was very white and the makeup she wore made it look hard as plastic. Her nose was straight and thin, her mouth strong and wilful. The low-cut black gown she wore did nothing to hide the magnificence of her body.

"Wyatt sent you?"

"That's bunk." He grinned at her. "I just wanted to get inside."

"What brings you out here?"

Hunter leered at her. "Desire."

Her eyes narrowed. She clenched her hand into a fist.

72

"Desire," he explained, "to see you. And, incidentally, to make a quick buck."

"Money." She relaxed as though back on familiar ground. "Tell me about it."

"All these months I've been away," he began, "you've haunted me. I can't get you out of my—"

"The money."

"I'd rather concentrate on you," he went on. "Your hair—"

"The money," she insisted.

"Just for once, Kiki, you ought to try to break down and be a woman."

"Being a woman is a business in itself. Kiki has other business."

"Too bad." His eyes prodded her body. "You certainly have the equipment."

"About the money?"

"Let it wait."

"Let the comedy wait. The money may be gone before you get back to it."

"Is that bad—if you have fun meanwhile?"

"With money you can buy fun."

"*You* can't," Hunter said meaningfully.

She shrugged, heedless. "Not now. But, when I'm ready . . ."

"You won't know what to do."

"A woman's supposed to operate by instinct, isn't she?"

"Instincts," he said, "are made to be obeyed. They atrophy when you ignore them."

The fencing was beginning to annoy her. He watched the shadow cross her face and a cold satisfaction illuminated his eyes for an instant, then disappeared.

"Maybe," she said, "Kiki just doesn't have the instincts. Or maybe—"

"Maybe there's just no money in them, eh?"

"Let's stick to the money, Hunter. That's an instinct we share."

"Well . . ." he began.

"If you've got something to say, say it."

His eyes slitted, focussed on her face. "Your junk business is about to be pushed over."

Her face went blank. Not puzzled, not bewildered. Just the blankness of complete muscular control. Even the shallow green eyes were momentarily opaque. "Junk?" she repeated.

"You know. Opium . . . morphine . . . marijuana . . . heroin. Just plain junk."

"I'm supposed to know what you're talking about?"

"Such a naive question." His laugh was openly scornful. "And all the time your eyes are as sharp as a pickpocket's."

"Keep talking," she said. "We'll pretend I know what you're referring to."

"Let's pretend the other way," he said drily. "We'll make believe you know nothing at all; that the kids smoking the reefers aren't your assets; that Westrope wasn't a name on your sucker list. Let's pretend that you're just an innocent victim of vicious gossip and that I'm wasting your very valuable time."

"Bravo," she said. Her eyes mocked him. "You're quite a moralist."

He started toward the door.

"Wait," she said sharply.

He stopped.

"Make your point. Without the dramatics."

His eyes gleamed. "All right, then. Distinctive Tobacco Products is being knocked over. Tonight."

"No!"

"Don't take my word for it. Find out for yourself."

She paced across the room in long firm strides, opened

the door to the outer office and said, "Get me Charlie." She picked up her telephone extension to wait.

When her connection was put through, she spoke sharply. "Charlie. Narcotics. Supposed to be raiding us. Tonight . . . I just got a tip . . . Yes, get me the dope . . . call back . . . Yes, at the club . . . Quickly." She hung up.

"I'll know in a minute," she told Hunter. "In the meantime, if you'd rather go out and watch the show while I wait . . ."

He shook his head. "Those customers of yours . . ."

Contempt gleamed in her emerald eyes. Her lip curled. "They get what they pay for. If it's bad for them, that's not my fault."

"An excuse also advanced by warmongers and pimps."

"And where do stool pigeons stand on your list?"

He bowed. "Touché."

The telephone shrilled. She picked it up. "Yes? . . . Yes, this is Kiki . . . They're *not*? . . . You're quite sure? . . . There couldn't be any slipup, it couldn't be done without," she looked at Hunter, decided not to mention the name, "your man knowing about it? . . . Good." She hung up.

He said, "Well?"

"There's the door, Mr. Hunter."

His smile was quizzical. It mystified her. She said: "Narcotics contemplates no action against me tonight. Or any other night, for that matter."

"Against *you?*" The smile teased her now. "Are you pretending you know what I meant?"

She opened the door. "Do you mind?"

He ignored her. "I came to make money."

"Unfortunately, you have nothing to sell."

"If it was straight," he wanted to know, "how much would you have paid?"

"Five hundred dollars."

75

"Five hundred!" He laughed. "For saving a hundred grand. You deserve to lose it."

"A thousand, then."

"You'll pay a grand?" He leaned forward.

His insistence was puzzling. "If you knew something . . ." She opened her hand. "But, I assure you, my pipeline to narcotics is . . ."

"Above reproach, you might say."

"At any rate," she said, with some exasperation, "no such action is contemplated."

"Who said anything about Narcotics?"

"I thought—"

"Yeah. And what do I care what you thought? I have the word. Will you pay a grand for it?"

"Really—"

His voice sharpened, snapped at her. "Don't haggle like a housewife at the butcher's. Will you pay?"

Her lips tightened. "Yes," she snapped back.

The gleam of satisfaction in his eyes was real now. He let her wait for a few moments, watched the angry flush seep over her face as she realized he was deliberately taunting her.

"Here's the lay," he said, just before she exploded. "Check it quietly. Don't mention my name. I don't want this botched."

"I assure you—"

"I don't want assurances. I want a grand."

"You'll get it."

"Good. Now—get on the phone. Check the D.A.; Inspector Grogan."

She frowned. "Where does he come in—"

He cut in quickly. "Politics. Murder. Westrope was a hophead. He was also a murder victim. He was also your

76

customer. This is an election fight. A raid is a spread in the sheets. It's publicity. Publicity means votes."

"But Mike Wyatt—" She bit the name off.

"It's all right, you can mention his name. You don't have to play footsie with me. I know about Mike. He owns the D.A. and you've bought Mike off. Okay, so call Mike and kill it. Go ahead."

He waited with impudent unconcern while she made six telephone calls trying to locate the politician. Finally, she slammed the phone into its cradle.

"He's out of town," she blurted.

"That's right—he blew. Powdered. And when he comes back, he'll tell you he knew nothing about it." His tone became heavily gibing. "He'll even apologize."

She scowled. He badgered her with more words. "In the meantime, this Grogan'll grab your whole stock. The papers'll scream for your hide. You'll be out a hundred grand. But don't feel bad—Mike'll come back and apologize."

Her eyes were suspicious. "What do you get out of this?"

He smiled. "One grand. No work. No sweat. Unless, of course," his voice became nasty, "you keep standing there mooning like a goddam biddy housewife while your cake is burning in the oven."

She snapped into sudden motion. Half a dozen strides carried her out of the room. The door slammed shut behind her.

Hunter grinned, took out a cigarette. His quick vibrant hands were shaking slightly as he tried to light it.

Kiki was back in three minutes. She sat down behind the desk, began to make out a check. He lifted the pen out of her hand.

His smile was bland. "No checks, please. Cash. Then I know I have it."

77

She buzzed her outer office. "Mike Wyatt'll know he has something, too," she promised grimly.

Hunter's face remained stiff and expressionless. Only his eyes grinned.

The man she had called "Charlie" on the telephone came into Kiki's office through a door that led directly to the parking lot of the club. A heavy, dark, perspiring man in his forties, he looked more like the minor executive of a small corporation than a gangster.

"Where've you been?" Kiki demanded, her voice a mixture of anger and tension. "We been waiting for you over an hour."

Charlie hesitated. "We . . . had trouble."

"Trouble? What kind of trouble?"

"Someone tried to hijack the truck."

"Hijack!"

"After we loaded the junk outta the store. Put two shots in the tires."

"Then what?"

"Nothing. They got cold feet. Took off. We couldn't follow on accounta the tires."

He sounded harried as he spoke, beset with difficulties that were too much for him. Kiki grimaced her irritation, then frowned at Hunter.

"There's one thing I don't understand," she said.

Hunter said, "Oh, sure, baby. I arranged the hijacking. I went to Mike Wyatt and told him to leave town. Then I put Grogan up to raiding you. After which, I came here and hung around so you'd be sure to have me to work out on after it was all over."

She shook her head, dissatisfied, but turned to Charlie. "What happened to the truck?"

"Rode it into the garage on the rims. The boys took the stuff and hid it out. They'll meet us later."

Kiki said, "Who fingered us with Grogan?"

"I don't know." Charlie frowned nervously.

"You're sure they're raiding us?"

"I don't know. All I know is they're raiding." He turned worried eyes up at her. "Who else would they raid?"

A man of about twenty-five came into the office through the outside door. A long scar etched an ominous angry line down his cheek from eyelid to jawbone. His face was hard, the mouth twisted disjointedly. There was a dangerous glitter in his eye.

Charlie's eyes grew wary. His manner discarded the petulant gestures. His voice grew firm. He said, "Took you long enough to get here, Lippy."

The man called Lippy spoke in a drawl. "I was in bed. A guy needs time to get out of bed."

"You'd make it faster," Kiki said sharply, "if you slept alone."

"I don't get paid to sleep alone."

"Poor Kiki," Hunter chuckled. "She still thinks it's better to sleep alone."

Lippy turned to Hunter. "Who the hell are you?"

"A snooper," Charlie shrugged. "A pigeon."

Lippy dismissed Hunter with a shrug. "What's the lay?" he asked Kiki.

Quickly, she told him of the impending raid and the hijacking of the truck.

"What happens to the fat shmears you pass out?" he demanded. "Is this what you get for your dough—raids?"

Charlie said: "Wyatt ran out."

"The louse."

"Fine state of affairs," Hunter complained, "when you can't trust a politician to stay honest about being crooked."

79

"What do we do?" Lippy wanted to know.

Kiki clenched her fist. The emerald eyes hardened. "I just spoke to the chief. We fight."

"How much fight?"

"Enough to fill your belly," she told him grimly. "Go out to the garage and check the hardware. We're going to need it."

Lippy grinned, swaggered out.

Charlie shook his head. "I think we ought to take a powder."

"No. We fight."

He spoke reasonably, convincingly. "We got a good setup here. Why risk it? Let the bulls have their raid. We'll lay low until after election, then go back into business."

"And what about the customers meanwhile? They go nuts. They crack. And, when they start screaming, there's no telling what'll happen."

He sighed. "You want it that way?"

"I want it that way." She scowled. "We pay Mike back tonight."

Hunter stood and started for the door. "I better go now," he said. "Lots of luck."

"Sit down," Kiki said sharply.

"I'd just as soon go."

Charlie said, with unexpected venom, "Sit down, stoolie."

Hunter turned to face him, bowed to the gun in Charlie's hand. "How touching." He grinned weakly at Kiki. "I didn't even know you cared.

"I love you, too," Charlie scowled. "Amost to death I love you."

"Spare me the affection."

"I ain't getting fat on it," Charlie pointed out.

Hunter said: "Just because your boss wouldn't do as you asked, don't warm your heater on me."

80

Charlie's dark face flushed. "Button up. Sit down."

Hunter met his eyes. He sat down.

Lippy came back. "Everything's just fine." The pupils of his eyes glittered and there was a moist shine on the whites. "Looks like good hunting."

"You like it, you do," Charlie said. "A nice fat pitch and you trigger-happy dopes have to go make fireworks out of it."

Lippy slapped the back of his hand against Charlie's stomach. "Getting soft, boy," he sneered. "You got a rep as a hard guy. But you're afraid of hardware." He jerked his head at Kiki. "Why, you got less guts than the dame."

There was a contemptuous edge to his voice. As if he was turning the knife in the wound of Charlie's cowardice.

The air in the room became tense. Charlie's eyes glinted and his face set into hard lines. He didn't look the minor executive any more. He looked like a man faced with the choice of confronting a menace or running from it. He looked as if he was advancing to meet it.

He put his hand into the pocket of his jacket. "In New York," he said bitingly, "I knew a guy like you. He was crazy. He always wanted to kill a cop. His name was Coll. *Mad Dog Coll.*"

Lippy's mouth twitched convulsively. His hand leaped across his chest, dived under his jacket.

The corner of Charlie's jacket lifted evenly, unhurriedly, leveled itself at Lippy's belly. Lippy's hand stopped at the shoulder holster in his armpit.

"C'mon out," Charlie taunted.

The twisted mouth contorted. "A sucker play?"

"I'm the coward," Charlie reminded him. "You're a tough guy."

"Not dumb, though. Not dumb enough to commit suicide. I ain't that dumb. I'm comin' out empty."

"Not facing me, you're not. Turn around."

"And take it in the back?" Lippy's voice scaled the heights of hysteria.

"Turn around. Bring your hand out empty and show me them both behind your back."

Lippy turned appealing eyes to Kiki. She was staring with ecstatic fascination. There was a look in her eyes like that of the thrill-crazed women at the fights, when they scream for a knockout.

She said, finally, "Do as Charlie says."

At the sound of her voice, Charlie's eyes flicked to her face. Lippy, watching, thought he saw a chance, jerked his hand out from under his coat. But he never got to use the gun.

Charlie jutted his chin. The gun in his pocket coughed three times. Lippy crumpled to his knees like a puppet whose strings had been cut. He pitched forward. The un-fired gun spilled out of his hand, bumped across the floor to Kiki's feet.

Charlie kept his hand on his gun, his gun on Lippy. Smoke wisping from the singed pocket, he bent over the body. With his free hand, he rolled the body of Lippy onto its back. Three crimson polka dots had blossomed in the bosom of the white shirt.

"He'll never get to kill a cop now," Charlie said thought-fully. He dropped the lifeless hand. It thumped against the floor.

Kiki's pent breath came wheezing out in a long sigh. There was a sparkle in her hard eyes. "We better dump him," she said. "Quick."

"This is one night," Hunter said drily, "that he'll sleep alone."

8

CHARLIE GRUNTED as he shouldered the heavy body and carried it out. Kiki toed the deep stain in the rug, the hard white mask of her face twisting malevolently. "Anybody waits for anything in this life is a damn fool. When you go, you go quick."

Hunter said: "Oh well, you'll dry clean the last of him away tomorrow."

"And damn good riddance." She kicked viciously at the stain.

"Interment will be private, of course?"

She didn't answer. Her jaw hardened as she followed her own line of thought.

Charlie came back, looking nervous and harried again. "You're sure," he asked petulantly, "that we have to fight this out?"

"Yes. And stop that goddam whining. You act like it's worse than a trip to the dentist."

"Okay," he said. "Let's do it and get it over with."

"You've worked out the details?"

Charlie outlined his plan of attack. "Mike and Jerry," he said quickly, "will duck around the back and hit 'em with some eggs. The boys and I'll lay out front and pick 'em off as they come out."

She said: "Call the chief and tell him about it. He wants to know."

"Where do I reach him?"

"My place."

He reached for the phone on her desk. She grasped his hand, lifted it away. "Not here." Her eyes shifted to Hunter. "Make the call outside."

Charlie was back in three minutes. "Let's go." Kiki went to the door. "You, too," Charlie said to Hunter.

"Wouldn't miss it for the world."

Kiki led the way to a massive black Cadillac, slid in behind the wheel. Hunter stopped beside the car. Charlie came up behind him, prodded his back with something hard and cylindrical.

"Up front," he said.

"I have my own car here."

"It'll be here when you get back."

"If you get back," Kiki added grimly.

"If I don't, I want you to have it," Hunter told her.

"Thanks."

"The brakes are so bad."

She jerked the vehicle away in a high-octaned rush of power that flung Hunter's back against the seat. His head rocked back onto his shoulders. The side of the road flew by in a blur.

After ten minutes, Charlie leaned over and pointed ahead. Kiki slowed down, nosed the car along, close to the side of the highway until she came to a dirt road. She turned into it, inched her way for several minutes, then stopped.

Charlie reached over, took the keys out of the ignition

switch and ran around to the back of the car. Through the rear window, Hunter saw him pull the lifeless body out of the trunk. He hoisted it to his shoulder, carried it off into the underbrush.

"He never even thanked you for the lift," Hunter remarked with casual irony.

Kiki turned to him. In the moonlight, her blanched face was rigid, strained.

"You look like a ghost with a tummy ache," he told her.

She twisted back and stared straight ahead.

"Why, Kiki," he marveled. "You look as if you're about to cry." He laughed. "What an ironic thought—imagine Kiki in mourning. Weeping."

Her teeth bit hard on her lower lip.

"Good-bye, old friend," he said. "Sleep well."

"Goddammit, shut up!" Her voice almost cracked.

He didn't say anything for a moment. The night noises seeped into the car. The soft sluff of the breeze. The irritating rasp of a cricket.

"Enough to give you the creeps," she grated. A muscle in her throat throbbed.

He cleared his throat. The harshness of the sound made her start.

She snapped her head around to face him. Her eyes were wide, staring. Her hand dove into the pocketbook, closed on the little gun. "If you make another sound . . ."

His hand darted out and switched the radio on. Dance music flooded the car. He turned the volume dial up until it was deafening, then gradually lowered it.

The stone mask that had been her face seemed to dissolve. "Thanks," she said. Her breath whistled out in a long sigh. "I came close to blowing my top."

He looked at the gun in her hand. "Came close to blowing *my* top, too."

85

She put the gun away. Charlie came back, the beads of perspiration glistening on his forehead. He stepped into the car, slammed the door shut.

"Let's step on it," he said. "The boys'll think we ran out on 'em."

Kiki gunned the motor, maneuvered the car into a U-turn and eased her way back in the opposite direction. Once back on the hard surface of the paved highway, she stepped on the gas.

Hunter held his breath and watched the speedometer needle make the slow circle of acceleration. Eighty . . . ninety . . . one hundred . . . and beyond . . . there was something savage in the way Kiki lashed the big mechanical brute toward the last limit of its capacity. As if the frantic hurtling was a sedative for her tension. As though, in the uncontained surge of power, she found a cathartic that cleansed her of the hysteria and terror.

Charlie put a restraining hand on her arm. "Take it easy," he said. "We're coming to the junction."

She knocked Charlie's arm away. The car slued across the road. She fought it with clenched jaw, righted it. Gradually—reluctantly, it seemed—she eased the heavy pressure on the accelerator. The big mechanical brute seemed to strain against her control. As if it wanted to sustain the pace.

As they approached the junction, Kiki blinked her headlights. Answering lights blinked back. Charlie nodded. "They're waiting for us."

Kiki stopped. Charlie ran out of the car, again taking the ignition keys with him. Two cars, each exactly like their own, were parked along the side of the intersecting road. Charlie approached each one, poked his head inside and spoke briefly to its occupants.

"All set, lead the way," he said as he came back. "Not too fast now. We're almost there."

86

The three car caravan made moderate speed in the same direction for another ten minutes. Then, Charlie plucked at Kiki's arm again, slowed her down. "Just ahead," he said.

"There it is," he said, a moment later.

It was a large square frame house, set back from the road in the middle of a cleared plot about two hundred feet wide. Growths of scrub trees bounded the clearing on both sides, running straight back from the road. A low hedge paralleled the highway across the entire frontage. There wasn't another house within miles.

Two hundred yards past the house Kiki killed the motor, the others stopping directly behind her. Men piled out and, in business-like fashion, went directly to the trunks and began to unload.

Heavy ammunition boxes were dragged out and pried open. A short fat man with ugly protruding eyes and a three-day growth of beard busied himself assembling a sub-machine gun. Two others began to deposit hand grenades in what looked like Boy Scout knapsacks. The rest fitted ammunition clips into army carbines.

"What an arsenal!" Hunter exclaimed.

"We picked it up here and there," Kiki said.

Hunter looked sidelong at the woman. "Not going along for the fun?"

"The chief gave specific orders she's to stay in the car," Charlie growled. "You stay with her and don't make no breaks."

He left them then, and went out to his invading army, issuing his orders in quick quiet tones. The two men with the grenades in their knapsacks hurried into the clump of trees beside the road. Straining his ears, Hunter heard the sound of their footsteps as they carelessly broke twigs and kicked rattling rocks.

"Silent as Indians," he said, to no one in particular.

87

The short fat man with the Tommygun was next to go. He bent low and sprinted along the road. At the point where the low hedge met the trees, he stopped and took shelter. He began to mount his weapon on a tripod, fixed its muzzle on the house, then lay down beside it.

Hunter turned his attention back to Kiki. She was watching the preparations with fascinated eyes.

"Mike's place?" he asked.

She nodded without shifting her gaze.

Two men, carbines slung over their shoulders, were laboring with a round heavy object. The others, carbines at ready, kept pace with them.

"What does Mike keep here?"

"Slot machines—hundreds of 'em. Roulette wheels. Dice tables. Other equipment. He bosses all the gambling in town, Mike does."

"Let's go up and watch the action," he suggested.

"You stick with me." Her hand went to her handbag.

"You don't want to miss it, do you?"

She hesitated.

"No breaks," he promised.

Excitement burned deep in her green eyes. "All right—but stay with me." She took the little gun out of her handbag and pushed it at his ribs. "Kiki means business."

He looked down at the gun. "Don't forget your knitting."

"Knitting?"

"Don't they always knit at executions?"

"Such literary sarcasm."

He shrugged and stepped out of the car. She followed, stepped on a rock and stumbled. He caught her arm as she was going down, yanked her erect.

"Thanks," she said.

"Don't bother. If you'd fallen, that piece would go off. It would probably have hit me."

"You think of everything, don't you?"

"I try to."

He led the way. She followed behind him until they were well into the thicket, then stepped up alongside. He turned left and walked until they came to the edge of the cleared plot.

The house was set back from the road about fifty yards. A line of trees extended from it to a two car garage about twenty feet away. A winding driveway twisted from the highway along which they came up to the entrance to the garage. Except for the hedge which paralleled the highway, the area was unobscured. A well-kept lawn sloped gently between hedge and house.

There were lights on in the upper story of the house. The shades were down. No shadows appeared on the shades to indicate any activity inside the house. It could have been deserted.

Charlie moved cautiously in the shadow of the hedge to the point where it broke for the drive. Alongside this opening, they had placed the heavy object Hunter had seen the two men carrying.

"Searchlight," Kiki explained. "Navy surplus."

Its operator was trying to focus it before he turned it on. As he swung it around, moonlight flashed off the upturned lens. In that instant, a shot snapped out.

Hunter threw himself to the ground. His sprawling feet banged against Kiki's legs, knocked her over. She landed heavily.

The sound of spilling fragments of glass from the searchlight lens reached his ears. "Score one for Mike's boys," he said grimly.

The Tommygun opened up, its fire lifting until the tracers rocketed against the house itself. A hoarse command from Charlie stilled its fire.

On the ground under the trees, Kiki exclaimed, "You're trembling!"

Hands shaking, Hunter admitted it. "Those are real bullets," he told her. "They frighten me."

The rattling echoes stilled. Silence seeped across the arena. They waited tensely.

"Where are those grenades?" Kiki asked tightly.

"That's what Charlie would like to know."

A blinding sheet of flame shot skyward. A deafening explosion followed. Then a second thunderous roar . . . a third . . . and a fourth.

The grenades had hit the house, at any rate.

Fire knifed up through the crashing timbers, slashed at the sky with its crimson blade. Charlie's men spewed steel-jacketed death across the lawn. Their very first volleys prodded the crumbling walls, nosed their menacing way inside the house.

There was no answering fire.

After several minutes, Charlie gave the command to stop. The flat splat of the carbine and the hysterical chatter of the Tommygun died away reluctantly. Slowly, their echoes were muffled.

Only the chuckling crackle of the flames remained. The fire waved mad flickering fingers of light on the scene.

Kiki looked at the house and snapped her fingers. "And that's that," she said. There was satisfaction in her voice.

Hunter's face was puzzled. He looked at her. His eyes slitted as he examined the house. He shook his head. His eyes shifted to the garage. He seemed to expect more.

Crouching low, Charlie and the others left the cover of the hedge and started cautiously toward the burning house. They spread out and, from the center of the rank, Charlie directed their progress in hoarse whispers.

The man at the Tommygun remained near the hedge.

After a moment, he got up off the ground and stretched his arms. He yawned, lighted a cigarette. By this time, the invaders were midway between the road and the burning house.

From the trees beside the garage came a volley of machine gun fire. The Tommygun operator reeled. He went down like a tackling dummy knocked loose from its moorings. The men on the lawn fell flat.

Two grenades came looping out to where they lay, landed on the lawn with a hollow thud. When they exploded, dirt and grass and mud and men flew in all directions.

Charlie stood up, began to stagger back toward the shelter of the hedge. A volley axed the legs out from under him. He sank to his knees, pitched forward to bury his face in the grass.

From the road, where the cars were parked, came more grenade explosions. The air they compressed whirred through the leaves. Overhead, the branches shook.

The firing ceased. There was no sign of motion on the lawn. The sounds echoed and re-echoed. The firelight flared higher. Hunter pressed his face closer to the ground.

Men issued from behind the trees near the garage. They stalked across the lawn slowly. At each fallen figure, they stopped, poured a stream of bullets into it, bent to feel it, to shake it, then walked on. From behind the house came the sounds of more gunfire, unreturned.

The wind shifted. Acrid smoke taunted Hunter's nostrils, jabbed at his eyes. He closed them, but the tears ran down his face. When he looked up, the men ranging the lawn had progressed down to the hedge at the highway.

The garage doors opened and two heavy cars shot out onto the twisting drive. At the highway, they stopped to pick up the men who had crossed the lawn. Then they careened onto the broad highway and disappeared.

In a moment, the lawn was empty. The only sound came from the fire gouging its way through the splintered timbers.

Beside him, for the first time since the action had begun, Hunter heard Kiki.

She was crying. Muffled, snarling sobs. She beat at the earth with her fists.

"Shut up," he hissed savagely.

She stood suddenly. "They're gone." Thoroughly, methodically, venomously, she cursed while her breath lasted.

"Get down, you damn wet hen. They may have left someone on guard."

"They knew we were coming," she panted. "All the time they knew."

"Psychic."

"It was a plant." The flickering firelight crimsoned her face. Her eyes glowed malignantly. The ugly little gun menaced him. "*You* planted it."

"Put that thing away."

She approached, stood over him. "Mike's boys got away. *You* won't." She raised the gun.

Hunter lashed out with his feet. His heels landed just below her kneecaps. She plummeted backward, the gun going off, its bullet going upward into the trees.

He followed after her. She fell backward, fought to rise. He kicked the gun out of her hand, knocked her down again. He picked up the gun, pointed it at her.

She sat there, snarling up at him. He spat words of explanation. "In the office all the time . . . right under your nose . . . had no idea of what you planned to do . . . couldn't have tipped anyone . . . 'cause you saw me every minute."

She stared at him, hard-eyed.

"Mike must have planned it this way from the start," he told her. "The only way it figures."

The baleful light faded out of her eyes slowly. Reason returned. She nodded. "Maybe."

"What other way could it be?"

"I don't know," she said. "I don't know."

9

ᘑᘔᘑᘔᘑᘔ

OUT ON THE LAWN, under the harsh illumination of the bloody firelight, someone began to moan. A thin, keening sound, low but penetrating.

Hunter looked down at Kiki. She turned her head away. The sound stopped.

He said: "That's one of your boys."

She didn't answer.

The sound came again. Soft and lonely, with the empty hopelessness of dying.

He said: "You ought to go out to him."

"Why?"

"He's dying."

"So?"

Hunter turned his back on her. He strode to the edge of the trees, looked out across the lawn. The moaning was very distinct now.

Hunter's thin lips twitched as if the sound caused him pain. His eloquent fingers closed and opened, closed and opened, as rhythmically as the pumping of a vein.

He turned to Kiki. "You won't go?"

She said: "*You* go to him."

He stared at her for a moment then, as though he realized it was useless to talk to her, turned and started toward the wounded man. He crouched as he crossed the lawn.

The man was lying on his back. His eyes were open and staring directly upward. If he was aware of Hunter's approach, he gave no sign of it.

Wordlessly, Hunter laid his hand on the man's forehead. There was no reaction, no sign of recognition. Hunter dropped to his knees and opened the wounded man's jacket.

The shirt underneath was a sodden mass of blood. In the dancing shadowy firelight, its color was alternately jet black and searing crimson.

The man's face was gray and his skin was cold. He was very near death. Hunter closed the jacket, prepared to go.

The man's hand moved. He said, softly, "Charlie?"

Silently, Hunter took the groping fingers in both his hands. The man swallowed, audibly. Hunter released the fingers. The hand fell to earth. The man closed his eyes. The only sign of life was the almost imperceptible rise and fall of the bloody shirt.

There was nothing left to do, no hope. Hunter turned and moved on to another motionless black blob fifteen yards further in toward the center of the lawn. This one was already dead. Before he had crossed to the other side of the clearing, Hunter had found and examined all six of the bodies of the men who had attempted to storm the house from in front.

They were all dead.

In the thicket on the opposite side of the lawn, Hunter turned to his right and silently made his way to the back of the house. Among the trees behind the house, he found two empty knapsacks. Near the garage, he found the riddled bodies of the two men who had started out with the grenades.

The garage had, so far, resisted the sparks that had fallen on it from the burning house. Hunter stood before its open doors for a moment, then went inside cautiously. It was empty.

He went back to where he had left Kiki. She was gone. He started toward the cars. After he had gone fifty feet, he found her, sitting with her back against a tree. She was smoking a cigarette.

"Well?" she asked.

"Every last one of 'em."

She dragged on the cigarette. Her face was impassive. After a while she said, "Took you so long. I thought you'd pulled out."

"How?"

"The same way we came."

He laughed at her.

She pretended to frown. "What's the matter?"

"Are you trying to tell me you didn't go back to the road to look at the cars?"

She didn't say anything.

"You went back there and you found nothing but junk." He ground his teeth angrily. "What do you think those grenade blasts behind us were? Just our cars being blown up."

"And I thought you stayed out of concern for poor Kiki?"

"You need my concern like a weasel in an unprotected henhouse."

"I'll get along," she admitted. She laughed mirthlessly. "What's the use of feeling sorry? The milk is spilled."

"Sister, that's not milk that's spilled out there."

"That's the racket." She plumed an impersonal feather of smoke into the air. "That's the racket. Come easy, go easy."

97

"Yeah."

She looked up at him, her eyes hard and calculating. "*You* wouldn't care to join Kiki in a nice, profitable pitch, would you?" She smiled. "I'm suddenly short of help, y'know."

"And end up like those boys out there?"

"It's quick dough. Lots of it."

"It has to be. You don't live long to spend it."

"Nothing ventured . . ." She lighted another cigarette. In the distance, a siren wailed mournfully, its sound approaching them. Her hand stiffened in the act of shaking out the match. "Who's that?"

His eyes turned to where the twisted bodies lay sprawled on the lawn, "Too late for an ambulance."

"The cops?" She stubbed the cigarette out. "Do we duck?"

"How? We have no car, no way of getting away. We'd only get picked up. Look better if we go right out to them." He stood. "Better let me do the talking."

Her eyes met his. "Okay." As he turned away, she heard him say, "This is all that was missing."

She frowned.

There was no mistaking the giant bulk that came looming through the hedge: it was Grogan. His eyebrows lifted when he saw Hunter advancing to meet him. It was a gesture more eloquent than if he had thrown up his hands.

Grogan leaned his big round dome of a head down to look at Kiki. Her jacket was smeared with mud; the skirt of her dress both smeared and torn. There was a bruise on her cheek she'd picked up when Hunter took the gun away from her.

Grogan stared at her. He tugged at his lower lip. "You're Kiki Morrison," he said.

"And who are you?"

"Grogan. Homicide."

"You're the guy who—" She broke off abruptly as Hunter jabbed his elbow into her ribs. She glared at Hunter, then turned to Grogan and said, "How interesting! I've always wanted to meet a real live inspector."

"I'll bet," Grogan said drily. He turned to Hunter. "And you?"

"Me?"

"Yes, you. Who are you and what in hell are you doing here?"

Kiki said: "Stop playing the heavy cop, Grogan. You're beyond city limits here. You're out of your jurisdiction."

"I'll worry about that," Grogan promised. "Some day."

Hunter said, "Miss Morrison and I were out for a drive when we saw the flames shooting—"

A uniformed patrolman came running up. "Stiffs galore out there in the grass, Inspector. Looks like a bloody stockyard."

Grogan wheeled with surprising agility. "Keep an eye on these two. If they break, smoke 'em. I'll have a look."

He hurried back to the highway. When he reappeared, he was on the running board of one of the police cars as it moved up the drive. The car veered to illuminate the lawn with searchlight and headlights.

Hunter looked at the square frame house. "The fire's dying," he said wearily.

Kiki said, "So it is."

They waited for Grogan to come back. Hunter shivered suddenly, as though aware for the first time of the chill of the night. He moved his arms and legs, felt the ache of his bruised body.

"Look at that," Kiki said drily.

He followed her eyes. The patrolman Grogan had detailed

to guard them had drawn his revolver and leveled it at them.

"He'll go far, this lad." Kiki's sarcasm was heavy. "Conscientiousness pays off."

The man flushed. "I was afraid it would look silly."

"There, there. Don't fret. Kiki understands."

Grogan came back, his granite features expressionless. "Looks like a massacre," he rumbled. "Frisk them," he ordered the patrolman who was guarding them.

The guard apologized as he put his hands in the pockets of Kiki's jacket. He seemed relieved when she said, "There's no inside pocket to the jacket. Although," she smirked, "you're welcome to look for one."

The patrolman shook his head hurriedly, shifted to Hunter. His eyebrows climbed as he found the small pistol Hunter had taken from Kiki. He handed the gun to Grogan.

Grogan hefted it. It seemed lost in the hugeness of his paw. With unexpected deftness, he broke it open, inspected it, smelled the barrel, then dropped it into his pocket.

"Been fired. When? Why?"

"Just a few minutes ago," Hunter explained. "I thought we might attract help that way."

Grogan sighed. "All right," he said wearily. "Gimme the whole story."

"Miss Morrison and I saw the flames shooting up into the sky and hurried over to see if we could help. But the house was deserted."

Grogan glowered. "That right?" he asked Kiki.

Her nod was indifferent.

"All right, then, what kept you here? Why didn't you get help?"

"That's the strangest part. While we were here looking for someone to help, we heard the motor of our car start up. By the time we ran back to the road, the car was gone. Of

100

course, I assumed that it was someone who'd gone for help. But—he never came back."

Grogan thrust his lower lip out contemplatively. Suddenly, his huge paw snaked out and cuffed Hunter on the side of the head. Hunter staggered back, regained his balance and started toward Grogan.

Another blow to the head met him and he reeled. Grogan pounced after him with ponderous speed, seized him by the coat lapels and lifted him off the ground. He shook the younger man like a terrier worrying a dead rat.

"Keep your eyes on the gal," he snarled over his shoulder to the patrolman. "I'm gonna see if maybe I can't make this guy do a little talking."

Two detectives hurried to the aid of their chief as he half-pushed, half-carried the squirming Hunter back toward the police car. Grogan bellowed them off, saying he had never needed help to handle rats like this before and, by God, he wasn't going to start now.

Back out of hearing of anyone in the party, Grogan asked fiercely, "Well, boy, what's the lay?"

Hunter spoke rapidly, sketching the events of the evening: his deception of Kiki; the attack; the ambush; the massacre.

Grogan pinched his lower lip reflectively. "All wiped out, eh? Is that good?"

"Couldn't be better," Hunter said quickly. "Kiki blames Wyatt. Wyatt'll throw a fit when he gets back. What more could I ask? Although," he admitted candidly, "I never expected all this when I started."

"I sure as hell hope you're right, boy. 'Cause if you're wrong . . ."

Hunter cut through the doubt. "Of course, I'm right. Did you pull that phoney raid?"

101

"Scupped a little piker over in the Black Belt. When we got back, there was an anonymous phone call that all hell was busting loose out here." He stopped, then said dubiously, "I'm still not sure how far I ought to ride along with you." He slapped Hunter on the side of the face. "The girl was watching us," he explained.

"You're in too deep to back out now," Hunter reminded him grimly.

"Lucky for you, too. I'm so scared, I might pull out and leave you high and dry." Abstractedly, he cuffed at Hunter again. "Dammit, boy, I thought my hands were quick but every time I throw one at you, you anticipate me and roll away from it. Why," he grumbled, "I ain't even mussed you yet."

Hunter grinned at him.

Grogan's face hardened. "You think you'll make it on this caper? You think you'll pull it off, boy?"

"I'm gonna try like hell."

"That sounds good, boy. Say it again. I want to see it in your eyes."

Their eyes met as Hunter repeated the words.

Grogan regarded him with steady seriousness. "I sure hope you do, boy." He grinned. His huge paw shot out suddenly and cracked hard against the side of Hunter's head three times in rapid succession. "Too fast for you that time, boy," he exulted.

Hunter shook his head. His ears were ringing. "Don't overdo it," he grumbled.

"You oughta look like you been roughed some more when you get back to that gal there. Besides," Grogan's chuckle rumbled as if it came out of a volcano, "you deserve a couple for that stinkin' story."

"I'd have done better if I had more time."

"Who do you figure squealed on their caper, boy?"

102

Walk the Bloody Boulevard

"I have an idea on that," Hunter admitted, "but I'm holding it back. But," he looked up at Grogan, "here's one I'll give you. It wasn't Kiki's crew that threw the grenades into that house; it was Mike's. You might go over that place with a fine-tooth comb when it cools down."

Grogan stiffened. "For what?"

"That concrete floor would make a lovely grave."

"We'll look into it." He stroked his massive chin. "I'm sending a car back to town to get the M.E. Wanna ride along?"

"Tell the driver to drop us at the Animal Fair."

Grogan nodded, then suddenly gave Hunter a violent shove. He followed after him and shoved all the way back to Kiki. Kiki did not seem at all displeased with the way her companion's features had been manhandled.

Her approval seemed to please the artist in Grogan.

The Animal Fair was deserted when the police car dropped them off. The lights were out, the building shuttered. The gravel crunched under Hunter's feet as he started toward his car, the only one remaining in the huge parking lot.

Kiki's hand on his arm stopped him. He turned, a question in his cold eyes.

She said, "I'd like to go inside first." Her hand indicated her muddy clothes. "Clean up and change."

"No one's stopping you."

"Will you wait?"

He scowled. "You could spend the night here."

"I . . . couldn't." Her face was tired. "I just couldn't."

"Then get a cab."

"Please." Her eyes were wide in appeal. The nails of the hand on his arm dug into his flesh. "*Please.*"

103

"I'm tired. Dog-tired." He hesitated, shrugged. "Okay."

He walked behind her. Stiffly, because the pain he felt and would not show seemed to rob his battered body of its natural pliancy.

She unlocked the door that led to her office. He started to follow, but checked himself. He waited outside until she had turned the light on. When he did go inside, he searched the room before he permitted himself to relax.

Neither spoke. Kiki opened a desk drawer and produced a bottle of Scotch, poured two stiff drinks. They drank greedily.

Kiki finished, put the glass down on the desk. "Now, if you'll excuse me." She took off her jacket.

He waved his hand wearily. The liquor seemed to have helped not at all. "Snap it up," he said.

There was a door behind the desk and she went through it now, closing it behind her. Soon, he heard the hiss of a shower. He rose slowly, began to look through the drawers of the desk. His fingers moved quickly, yet without neglecting the smallest scrap of paper, but nothing there seemed to merit a second glance.

He went back to the sofa and stretched out on it. His face was gray. The deep shadows under his eyes gave them a haunted look. After a moment, the pain of his ribs forced him to change the position of his body.

Just as he had leaned back again, he sat up sharply as though a sudden thought had alarmed him. He walked to the door and switched the lights out. From there, he went to the window and stared searchingly across the empty expanse of the parking lot. He could see nothing.

He went back to the couch. After a while, the noise of the shower stopped. His fingers lifted themselves, curved into a position of alertness.

It was dawn now and the first milky light had begun to

104

gray the room. Behind the desk, he heard Kiki open the door but he did not move. It was as if the fatigue he felt had robbed him of all motility.

He sensed, rather than heard, her approach from behind. His hands stiffened. He started to sit up. By then, she had circled the couch, was pressing him back.

He suffered himself to be pushed back. Her nakedness was cool to his hand. His fingers moved sensuously on her flesh, barely touching it, yet seeming to drink deeply.

Her body barely rested against his. Her lips went to his flirtingly. A coquettish peck that was a caricature of chasteness.

His fingers tightened on her flesh. Then suddenly, as though she herself had lost control of the game she had initiated, her mouth opened. It pressed smotheringly on his kips. Her arms constricted around his neck. He could hear the hot breath hissing out through her nostrils.

He sat up with violent abruptness. The sharp movement sent her sprawling.

"Can the games, Kiki," he snarled. "Get some clothes on and let's get the hell out of here." He stalked out to the car to wait for her.

The ride back to town was silent. At her apartment, he went around and opened the car door for her. In the lobby of the building, before he could go, she said, coolly, "That offer I made you back there was on the level."

"I thought you'd renounced being a woman."

"I'm not going to work at it."

"But you'd like to play, eh?"

"When the playmate intrigues me."

He said nothing.

She said, "Why not come up?" The hard green eyes taunted him.

He shook his head.

"I'll be good," she promised. "Won't even try to show my etchings."

He hesitated.

"Just for a drink."

He wavered. She took his arm. Her finger indicated her name in the apartment listing. "This door's open for you. Anytime. Apartment 9K." She jabbed lightly at the bell, half-smiling as she did so. "Let's have a drink."

He broke away. "Good night, Kiki."

Her eyes darkened in speechless anger.

His lips writhed furiously. He raised his fist as if to strike her. She quailed at the storm on his face.

He lowered his hand. He smiled, a smile that was deadly. "Good night, Kiki," he said.

His eyes seemed barely able to stay open as he drove home. He staggered as he crossed the pavement to his own house. He had to hold onto the wall as he opened the door.

Once inside, he reeled into the bedroom. His face twisted in a grimace of pain, he collapsed onto the bed. His fingers were still fumbling with the buttons of his shirt when he lost consciousness.

10

IT WAS NOON of the following day, Saturday—the fifth day after the disappearance of Samuel Williams—and Peter Hunter was at breakfast when Tim Moloney came in. Tim followed Hunter into the kitchenette.

"Coffee!" Moloney exclaimed unbelievingly. "I thought you private eyes never drank anything less than a hundred and fifty proof."

"Careful—don't let Humphrey Bogart hear you. I'd be disgraced." He saw the newspaper protruding from Moloney's jacket pocket. "Gimme," he said.

The skinny blond man handed it to him. Hunter spread the paper. The scarehead across the top screamed: GANG WARFARE FLARE-UP. The story went on to tell of how the police, in answer to a mysterious telephoned tip, had discovered the riddled corpses of eight men, apparently slaughtered in a gun duel beyond the city limits. For the edification of THE SENTINEL's readers, each corpse was minutely described down to the last bullet hole. At the time this edition had gone to press, the police had been unable to crack the case, although their investigation indicated several promising theories.

Hunter grunted, sipped at his coffee. "They're going to lay low on it," he said.

"You know about it?"

"Yeah."

"But you're not telling, eh?"

"No." He met Tim's eyes. "Better for you if you don't know."

"Oh." Tim's eyes softened. "You look like hell," he said gently. "How's the ribs?"

Hunter touched his side, winced. "Lousy."

"The doc said—"

Hunter cut him short. "I'm not interested."

"Suit yourself."

Hunter gulped the last of his coffee. He poured another cup, hot and black. " 'Nother?" he asked Tim. Tim shook his head.

Hunter said, "What about Wyatt? He come back?"

"Early this morning. By plane. Then he slipped out of the airport and hotfooted it to Mayor Burkett's home."

"Burkett! But Kennedy's his man."

"Or *was*."

"I see what you mean."

Tim opened the paper to an inside page. "Take a look at this." His bony finger indicated the first column.

SPECIAL PROSECUTOR NAMED, the headline said.

"So that's why Mike Wyatt went to the governor," Hunter mused.

"What else?"

"And that's why he's back with Burkett now."

Tim grimaced. "Uncle Mike is throwing Kennedy overboard."

"That's obvious. But, tell me this." he leaned toward Mo-

108

loncy and his voice became grave, "why should Burkett go back with Mike? Especially when he must know Mike's in difficulty?"

"Search me. Honor among thieves, maybe."

Dissatisfied, Hunter shook his head. He turned back to the newspaper, began to read the statement of the special prosecutor.

"With the announcement of the disappearance of Samuel Williams, veteran and highly respected city chemist, there is no longer any doubt that a vicious scandal is at the point of being exposed. During the past week, this city has witnessed the violent death or mysterious disappearance of three figures prominent in the business of public construction. Also, within that same period, one of our foremost contractors has taken his own life.

"I have in my possession" (the prosecutor went on) "some astonishing evidence, evidence which is even now in the process of evaluation and authentication by my staff. If, as now seems probable, certain hypotheses are true, then the very foundations of the construction industry in this city will be shaken down to bed rock.

"It is too early to make predictions. But I issue this warning to the malefactors: the law cannot be flouted with impunity. As special public prosecutor, I am fully cognizant of the grave responsibility entrusted to my care. I shall exert every effort to see that those responsibilities are properly discharged. The guilty will be punished."

Tim said, "He's an ambitious guy. He wants to be the state's attorney general next year. He's going to try to ride in on this case."

109

Hunter threw the paper aside and went into the living room. He sat down. His eyes went to the ceiling. His fingers rubbed each other.

"Oh, there's one thing I forgot," Tim said. "I found a girl who was in Spero's bar the night Kennedy met Williams there."

Hunter waited for more.

"For enough dough, she'll talk about who else was there."

"You think she knows anything?"

"She might. She used to be Chuck Byron's girl friend."

"Mike's killer, eh?"

"She might know something."

Hunter nodded. "I want to see her."

His eyes went back to the ceiling. Presently, he said, "Tim, let's go over it all, from the beginning. Let's see if we can get a pattern out of it now."

Tim nodded.

"In the beginning," Hunter said, "Samuel Williams called Kennedy, said he wanted to talk to him."

"And, although Kennedy denies it, he did have the meeting with Williams—"

"Whereupon, that very night, Williams disappeared." Hunter stopped, looked down at his hands. "Kennedy called me in to find him. He lied to me."

"About meeting Williams. About Blake being in Canada, too."

"He went to Harrison Barclay, Kennedy did, and told him Williams had made tests showing that the concrete used in paving the Belt Boulevard had been deficient. Barclay replied by committing suicide. Oddly enough, the allegedly wealthy contractor died almost penniless."

"It would seem," Tim surmised, "that Williams was right . . . that he was either kidnapped or killed because of it."

"Check. Now, I went after another chemist named West-

110

rope who was the official tester of materials for the job. West-rope got the wind up and called Kennedy's office after seeing me. He tried to leave the country, was murdered before he could do so."

"And," finished Tim, "a guy named Malbin, who also worked on the Belt Boulevard was killed, too. On his way, I learn, to tell the police what he knows about Williams."

"Finally, Tim, Kennedy and Mike Wyatt quarrel—if Peg is to be believed, and I believe her. Wyatt goes to the governor—and gets a special prosecutor."

"And, when he gets back, he goes into conference with his opponent, Mayor Burkett."

Hunter leaned forward. "Shall I tell you why?"

"Tell me."

"Because they're going to pin these murders on George Kennedy." He leaned back. "Yessir, Timmie, the whole set-up's about to blow skyhigh. With the blast being detonated under George Kennedy."

Tim smiled indifferently. "So what?"

"Meaning what, Timmie?"

"Far as I can see, Kennedy and Burkett are as alike as Tweedledee and Tweedledum. So what difference does it make if Kennedy's indicted and Burkett wins?"

Hunter lifted a finger solemnly. "Take it with me, Tim. Let's take it slow, though."

"Shoot."

Hunter bent an angular finger. "First, Mike is about to throw Kennedy to the wolves. Which brings up the second point." He bent another finger. "What made Mike pick Kennedy in the first place? Because you and I know Mike wouldn't take anyone he couldn't control, don't we?"

"You tell me."

"Okay." The third finger went down. "Mike's known about this crooked paving deal all the time. He's known the

111

firm of Kennedy and Blake was involved. He's been sure that, when the going got tough, he could jump Kennedy through a hoop by threatening to expose him."

"So?"

"So Mike's been surprised. Kennedy's told him to go to hell. Which means," he ticked the last finger off, "that it's just possible that Kennedy is an all right guy after all."

"How do you propose to find out?"

"Find out?" Hunter stood abruptly. His eyes closed in pain momentarily. He put his hand to his ribs. "Find out, Timmie?" he said, after a moment. "We're going down to jump George Kennedy over the coals."

Peg Wyatt looked up from the typewriter when the two men entered her office. A shadow curtained her eyes momentarily at the sight of Hunter. She said, "Yes?" and her voice was utterly uninflected.

Hunter said, "I thought you'd be *glad* to see me."

"I'm thrilled. I have to fight to hold it back."

He grinned. "Relax. I understand. Boss in?"

"Reading the papers."

"See if he'll see us."

She went inside, was back in a moment. "Go right in."

Hunter said, "Timmie, go ahead. I'll join you in a moment."

Moloney frowned, but went. Hunter turned to the girl. Her face was expressionless as she waited for him to speak. Her eyes were as bottomless as the sea.

He said, "About last night—"

She didn't blush as she interrupted. "Let's not speak of last night. I'm trying to forget it."

"I'm not," he said quickly.

Her smile was unexpectedly dazzling. An eager look lighted her face. She started to speak, then checked herself

112

Walk the Bloody Boulevard

suddenly. Finally, she said, "Mr. Kennedy's waiting for you."

"I'll be back," he said, and went inside.

Kennedy rose with the paper in his hand as he entered. "It doesn't look good, does it?"

"The depths of understatement," Hunter said drily.

Kennedy's attempt at a smile was boyishly wry.

Hunter said: "Kennedy, I want some straight dope."

The engineer bridled. "Straight dope?"

"Don't get sore at me. You're in a jam, man. You need every friend you can find."

"And that includes you?"

"If I'm satisfied you're leveling."

Kennedy thought a moment, then said, "Shoot. I'll answer your questions."

"What made Wyatt think he could control you?"

"I don't know." Kennedy squared his shoulders. "Anyone who thinks he can control me is in for a horrible surprise."

"What about the Belt Boulevard job?"

Kennedy jutted his jaw pugnaciously. "What about it?"

"What about it?" Hunter's laugh was ugly. "The job was rotten. The city's been robbed on it. You know it."

The engineer's teeth bit hard on his lip. "I don't know a thing. All I know is—if it was rotten—I never got a cent of any dirty money."

"How about Jim Blake?"

"I don't know."

"Where is he?"

"In Canada."

"That's a lie," Hunter snapped. "The airport has no record of his leaving. The trains show no reservation in his name."

Kennedy clenched his fist. "It may be wrong—but it's *not* a lie. He told me he was going to Canada. That's all I know."

113

"Okay, you don't know. Let me ask something else. You think Jim Blake was involved in this?"

Kennedy turned away. It was as if it was a question he didn't want to face. He put his hand on the desk. He said, softly, "He had to be, didn't he?"

"Why?"

There was anger in Kennedy's face. "A supervising engineer knows everything on his job." Pain etched its pattern in his face. "For God's sake, don't you see what this means? My own partner—more than that, my *friend*—turns out to be a louse." The thought of the treachery seemed to overwhelm him.

There was silence. Finally, Hunter said, gently, "Kennedy."

The engineer looked up.

"What did you and Mike quarrel about?"

"Montgomery. Mr. Wyatt wanted me to announce his appointment."

"And you refused?"

"I told Wyatt there was no room for Montgomery in my housing program. I told him I really wanted housing for those veterans."

"And Mike threatened you with the Belt Boulevard scandal?"

Kennedy's face showed surprise. "Why no—he never mentioned it."

"*Didn't mention it!*" Hunter's hands jumped convulsively. "No."

"He didn't try to bully you, to steamroller you?"

He shook his head. "He didn't argue. It was more as if he was offering me one last chance to cooperate. When I refused, he just dropped the subject."

Hunter stood up, paced the room excitedly. The others

114

watched him narrowly. The detective turned and said: "It figures only one way."

They waited for him to elaborate.

"Mike thought he could jump Kennedy through a hoop, but he didn't even try. He ran, instead, to the governor. When he got back, he went to Burkett. Why should he put himself in the hands of a guy he knows has no reason to love him?"

The silence was absolute.

"There's only one possible reason: *Because they're both involved themselves!*"

"Wyatt? And Burkett?"

"If it was only Wyatt, he'd never go to Burkett. It must be both."

Kennedy nodded slowly. "It *could* be that way." He was about to say more when Peg Wyatt came in with a newspaper in her hand.

"I thought you'd like to see this," she said excitedly. "It's an extra." She spread it out over the desk.

MISSING CHEMIST DEAD
WILLIAMS BODY FOUND IN GUTTED BUILDING

"Police probing the smoking ruins of the building at the sight of last night's sensational gang battle announced at noon today that they had discovered a body which is unmistakably that of Samuel Williams, the chemist who has been missing since last Monday.

"While no further details are available, it is understood that the body was found in the concrete basement. . . ."

"That place of Mike Wyatt's," Hunter said. "I was sure they had something buried there. They threw the grenades

115

into it themselves because they wanted the body found."

Peg said, quickly, "It says here that the attempt to trace the ownership of the building has bogged down because the owner's name and address, as listed on the tax rolls, turned out to be fictitious."

Hunter said, "Such loyalty, kitten." She flushed at the sarcasm in the words.

Kennedy slammed his fist on the desk. "Someone is going to pay for this," he said with quiet fury.

They looked at him amazed. The sudden outburst of temper was completely out of character.

"I knew Samuel Williams," he said. "There never was a finer, more upright man. He was killed because of what he'd uncovered."

An exclamation from Tim turned their attention back to the newspaper. He was pointing to a bulletin obviously inserted at the last moment.

MAYOR PROMISES EARLY ARREST

"Mayor Burkett announced, as this edition went to press, that the identity of the figure behind the latest wave of murders in the construction industry would be announced soon.

" 'We don't want any small fry,' Mayor Burkett said. 'We want Mr. Big, the man who caused it all. And we'll have him within twenty-four hours.' "

Hunter turned to Kennedy. His hands made a harsh strangling gesture. " 'Mr. Big!' " He rasped. "That means you!"

II

"YESSIR," HUNTER snapped, "you're the boy he's voting for. They're measuring you for the noose right now."

"Hang me?" Kennedy's eyes were shocked. "Dammit, man, how can they hang me when I'm innocent?"

Hunter started to laugh, stopped with the sound still in his throat. "Your partner isn't, though," he explained gently. "Therefore, your firm's involved and that's enough to make a case. Blake's missing and that in itself is a confession of guilt. Then, after they've blackened you on the paving fraud, they'll tie you to one of these murders. It won't be hard. Perjured testimony comes cheap."

"But they can't do it. I'm innocent."

Peg said: "It'll be easy for Uncle Mike."

Kennedy looked at her sharply. She met his eyes coolly. "He's done it before," she explained.

"Then we've got to find Jim Blake. He can clear me."

Hunter shook his head. "Even that wouldn't help. If he took the blame—and he wouldn't—they'd say you paid him to be the fall guy. You might not be convicted, but you'd certainly be ruined. Burkett would lick you hands down."

"Good God," Tim exploded. "Don't make it sound so damn hopeless."

"I'm sorry, Timmie. But that's the way it is."

Peg said: "You'll just have to kill Uncle Mike."

They looked at her, all three. Hunter laughed. "That would be a solution."

"Don't you see? Uncle Mike is trying to kill you. What else can you do?"

"You can't be serious, Miss Wyatt."

"But there's no other way," she said. She sounded as though she was lecturing children. "You can't fight a tank with moral scruples. And Uncle Mike's as ruthless as a tank. You have to fight him his way. And, if what you're fighting for is worthwhile, it doesn't much matter how you beat him."

Kennedy said angrily, "I won't do it."

"Then he'll make mincemeat of you."

"If he's involved in the paving fraud, we'll prove it," Kennedy said.

"He's too clever for that."

Hunter looked at Peg keenly, then turned to Kennedy. "If it would help to overcome your reluctance, I can tell you Mike killed Williams."

"And many, many others," Peg added.

"I won't be a party to murder and that's final," Kennedy said. "If Wyatt's a killer, then let the law take over."

"Well, then," Tim said hopelessly, "all we have to do is pin a murder rap on him."

Peg smiled thinly. "And ask him to stand still while you're doing it."

Hunter said, "I don't know. We might as well try. It's our only hope."

118

She looked at him sharply. "And how do you suppose you're going to do that?"

"What's your plan?" Kennedy asked.

"Tim and I will try to muddle it through."

"And what do I do?"

"You stay here. I'll call on you if I need you."

Kennedy's face fell. "I hate to have you out alone," he said earnestly. "Fighting my battle while I do nothing to help."

"That's the best way," Hunter said laconically.

"Why, the police will be here to arrest me soon."

"Burkett'll probably wait a while. He's hoping you'll figure this out. He wants you to make a run for it."

"I'm staying here."

"Good. Flight would only make you look that much guiltier." He looked around the room. "Okay, Timmie, let's go."

Peg Wyatt went out to the outer office with them. "You'll be careful?" she asked Hunter softly.

He smiled. "Very."

She said, "I can't forget last night either." Her eyes were soft: her lips trembled. "I don't want to."

Out in the street, Tim said, "Is it as hopeless as you made it out upstairs?"

Hunter's face was grave. "For us it's even worse."

"Why?"

"Because we're staking everything on the hope that Kennedy's on the up-and-up. And this whole thing may be nothing more than a falling out among thieves."

"Of whom Kennedy may be one?"

"Exactly."

"So what do we do?"

"Just stick with me, Timmie. I'm going to pick up Jim Blake."

Five minutes later, they stood outside an apartment door. The number on it was 9K. Hunter jabbed his finger at the mother-of-pearl button.

Soft chimes sounded inside. "Ready?" he asked Tim.

Tim's hand tightened on the gun in his pocket.

A woman's voice inside asked, "Who is it?"

Hunter leaned close to the jamb. He muffled his voice with his hand. "From Mike Wyatt," he said.

The door inched open slowly. Hunter put his shoulder against it and shoved. The woman inside was knocked off her feet.

"Sorry, Kiki." He smiled as he bent to help her up. "Animal spirits. Friendly as a puppy when I see an old friend."

Her venomous eyes looked startlingly green. Her teeth grated against each other audibly.

"You know my partner, Tim Moloney? No?" He went through the formality of an introduction. His eyes were glued on her face.

Her glance raced past him to the closed door through which they'd entered. An angry frown indicated she was seeking furiously for a way out of a dilemma.

"Get out," she said finally.

"Just a pair of friendly visitors, Kiki. Do invite us in."

"I . . . can't."

"No?"

"There's someone inside." She tried to giggle, but the sound came out hollow.

"Naughty, naughty." He waggled a chiding finger at her. "But your eyes are worrying about the door, not the bedroom. You're afraid someone might blunder in."

"That heavy brain ought to make you round-shouldered."

120

"Don't be coy, Kiki. Ask us in." His quick finger jabbed at her midriff. She fell back.

He started into the apartment, Tim behind him. Sudden anger flushed Kiki's face. She tore at him, scratching. He picked her up bodily. Her kicking and writhing made absolutely no impression on him.

He set her down in the living room, looked around. The room was done in Chinese modern, the conventional cherry and black. There was a huge mirror over the sofa. The lamps were twisted nudes of some jade-like substance. It looked like a carbon copy of a magazine picture.

"How soon do you expect Jim Blake, Kiki?" he asked.

Her answer was to tighten her lips.

"You must expect someone or you wouldn't be so worried about the door."

She remained silent.

"The way I figure it, Blake has been living here all the time he was allegedly in Canada. I figure him as the boss of your junk combine." He stopped, shot a sharp glance at her. "How'm I figuring, Kiki?"

Her mouth twisted sourly. "You're so smart—answer your own questions."

"It's easy enough to prove." He turned and went into a bedroom.

Kiki stood up, started to move toward the door. Tim said, "Sit down, Kiki." He planted himself before her.

Her eyes met his as she estimated the possibilities of evading him. Tim said, "Be a nice girl. Sit down."

She sat down.

Hunter came back carrying a man's sport jacket, tan with a bright overlay of a blue plaid. "I take it this is Jim Blake's, Kiki."

She didn't answer.

[21]

He said: "By the way, Kiki, how does it feel to live with a guy who tried to kill you? You *do* know that Jim Blake tried to kill you, don't you? Remember—Charlie called him last night before we went out to Mike's place. He told Jim just how he planned to attack the place, too. And what did Jim do? He tipped Mike's boys. And he ordered the special grenades for the cars. He was very explicit about that, remember? We were not to leave the cars, were we?"

Kiki kept her face expressionless. Not a muscle moved. It seemed a matter of complete indifference to her.

"And then you tried to seduce me up here last night. You figured you'd get me into the apartment hanging onto your lips and there'd be gunplay. Was he to kill me, Kiki, or vice versa? Tell me, did you have any preference?"

"I was hoping it would be both."

Before he could answer, the door chimes rang softly. Tim looked up questioningly.

Hunter moved to Kiki's side. His hand covered her mouth before she could scream. She sank her teeth into the flesh of his palm. He swore softly, hung on grimly.

His voice was softly tense. "Take your gun, Timmie and answer the door. Bring whoever's there inside. And—make sure you're still the boss when you bring him in."

Tim's nod was matter-of-fact. His hand came out of his pocket holding an automatic. He disappeared into the foyer.

There was a muffled grunt of surprise at the door . . . then, the soft padding of footsteps across the carpeted foyer. When the two men came in, Tim was in the rear, his hand prodding the gun into the other's back.

Satisfaction flamed in Hunter's eyes. The thin twisted smile of his lips was cruel. It showed the wolfish teeth.

Hunter said, softly, "Mr. Blake, I'm very happy to see you."

122

Walk the Bloody Boulevard

Jim Blake was floridly handsome. He had a wide, sen-suously-lipped mouth. His nose was full and straight, his eyes deep and brown. His hair was thinning, but he had combed it carefully to hide the incipient bald spot.

His clothes were expensive, carefully cut and too care-fully warm. The fleecy natural-colored camel's hair topcoat had a pile deep as a Chinese rug. Beneath it, a chocolate tweed jacket paired itself with faintly green gabardine slacks. His shirt was pale green and, on his bow tie, horizontal stripes of green and chocolate alternated.

With a pair of binoculars slung over his shoulder, he might very well belong in the owner's circle on Derby Day at Churchill Downs.

He walked in with his head high, giving the impression of ease. But his eyes darted here and there, always roving, never stopping. He looked at Hunter . . . then at Kiki . . . then back to the gun in Tim's hand.

He looked into the mirror and his attention fixed there. He stopped to tug his bow tie absolutely horizontal. He straightened his lapels. He adjusted the handkerchief in his breast pocket.

When he turned away from the mirror, his eyes started roaming again. They twisted from Kiki to Hunter to Ken-nedy, made the circle again.

Hunter said: "I'm Hunter—Peter Hunter. And this is Tim Moloney. We've been looking for you."

Blake's voice was easy, rich and warm. "I've heard of you." His eyes flicked at Hunter, then jumped to Tim.

"You certainly did." Hunter laughed mirthlessly. "I'm the guy you tried to rub out the other night. No, no—" he said as Blake tried to interrupt "—don't sing me sweet music. You arranged that party for Kiki's boys. I *know* you did."

Blake twisted the button of his jacket. His hand went up

123

to follow the course of his carefully combed hair. "Some-one's been giving you a party," he said derisively.

"Someone tried to. You."

Blake shrugged. If he feared the gun in Tim's hand, his face didn't show it. He sat down gracefully, but didn't take the fleecy topcoat off.

Impatiently, Tim demanded, "What about the Belt Boulevard job?"

"What about it?" Blake asked confidently. "It's all finished, that's all."

"Finished, yes," Tim snapped. "But how? What about the deficient concrete? The overpayments?"

He gestured angrily with the automatic as he spoke, scarcely realizing that he still held it.

Blake looked at the weapon. "Better put that away, son," he said pointedly, "before you hurt yourself with it."

Hunter rose, stood over the engineer. "You're pretty sure of yourself, aren't you?" he rasped. The thin lips curled back from the wolfish teeth in a snarl.

Blake smiled. "I am."

"Mike Wyatt's behind you and you know that. And you think Mike can square anything, don't you?"

This time Blake merely smiled.

"So you're sure that all you have to do is wait and everything will be all right."

Blake shifted his position easily. "You're like a couple of kids playing ping pong with a bomb. You think you're having a lot of fun." He smiled easily. "Pretty soon the bomb'll go off. And you—" He snapped his fingers contemptuously.

Hunter took the gun from Tim's hand. He bounced it up and down in his palm. He walked over, sat down beside Blake. Tim's eyes narrowed.

Blake said, "And that popgun doesn't scare me either."

124

"Tell us about the paving job," Hunter demanded. "Who was in on the split?"

Blake ignored the question.

Hunter's face was absolutely wooden. Only the bunched muscles at the hinge of his jaws showed his tension. Those, and the blaze in the cold blue eyes.

"Tell us," he said softly.

"I've already said—"

Hunter smashed the barrel of the gun across the bridge of Blake's nose.

"Damn you—tell us!"

Blood gushed out. It flooded down Blake's chin, dripped onto the fleecy coat. The nose spread flat across the engineer's face, as though the cartilage had been steamrollered.

Kiki sucked her breath sharply. Her eyes searched Hunter's face. She cringed from the cruelty in the ferociously cold eyes.

Tim nodded matter-of-factly. It was as if he had expected this all the time.

Blake jerked clutching fingers up to cover his face. Hunter snatched at the hands, tore them away from the engineer's face. Blake stared at the blood on them, horrified.

"Well?" Hunter's flat voice lashed at him. The engineer didn't answer. Hunter rapped furiously at his arms and shoulders with the gun. Blake hunched over, turtled under his arms and elbows to protect his head.

Impatiently, Hunter tossed the gun to Tim. He stood, reached down and grasped Blake's collar, twisted it. With one hand, he yanked the man to his feet. He pulled Blake's face close to his.

"Well?" he snarled, and the fury blazed uncontrolled in his eyes. "Do you talk?"

Mutely, Blake stared at him.

125

Hunter twisted the collar, shook the engineer. "Well?"

The engineer nodded dumbly.

Hunter stared at him, shoved hard. Blake sat down heavily. His head rocked back and forth on his shoulders.

Hunter turned to Tim. "We got to get him outta here. Some place we can take down what he says. Mike may come in here any time." His eyes searched the room, rested on Kiki. "And, we've got to fix *her* so she doesn't give the play away."

Kiki cowered from him. Terror made her eyes look like ground glass.

Hunter said, "Tie her up and let's get the hell out of here."

At Hunter's direction, Tim parked the car behind the building. They went up in the self-service freight elevator.

It being Saturday afternoon, the offices were deserted. They went through quietly: Tim in front, followed by a dazed, bleeding Jim Blake, with Hunter bringing up the rear.

Peg Wyatt was still sitting at her typewriter. The sight of Blake's face shocked her. The three men brushed by her, went into Kennedy's office.

Kennedy stopped in the midst of pacing the floor. His eyes widened at the sight of his partner. "What happened?" he asked.

"Your partner's had a little accident," Hunter said laconically.

Blake nodded mutely. His face, streaked with blood, was abnormally pale.

Peg came in with a first aid kit. She moistened absorbent cotton at the water cooler, began to sponge the blood from Blake's face.

126

"Has anyone called a doctor?" she asked.

"Don't bother, kitten," Hunter told her. "We haven't time."

"But—"

"We'll take care of it later."

Blake began to move his lips. "See," Hunter said, "he's coming out of it."

Blake began making an attempt to spruce his clothes. He stared at the blood on his coat, tried to wipe it off. His hands shook.

Hunter said: "Get your coat, kitten. I've got a job for you."

She stopped her ministrations to Blake. Her eyes sought Hunter's inquiringly.

"Blake here's agreed to tell us all about the Belt Boulevard pitch. We'll need a stenographer to take it all down."

"Miss Wyatt!" Kennedy exploded. "Why involve her in this mess. She's a woman—"

Hunter interrupted drily. "The age of chivalry is dead. How 'bout it, kitten? Like to be in at the death?"

The last word stilled the smile she had started. "At the death?" she echoed.

"A figure of speech. Are you with it?"

"I'll go."

Kennedy reached for the phone. "I'll get one of our male stenographers. A good one, too—"

"Kitten knows the whole pitch. Why bring in a stranger?"

"It's wrong to involve her—"

"There's no choice."

She said, "Please—I'd *like* to go."

"I thought you would." Hunter smiled at her. Only his eyes remained cold. They seemed to be mulling something in the future. Far in the future.

Kennedy said, "Very well. I'll get my coat and—"

"You'll have to stay here," Hunter said.

Kennedy stared at him, too astonished for words.

"We're getting a statement that will exonerate you," Hunter explained. "You have to be as far away as possible when we get it. That way, there'll be no possibility of coercion on your part."

"Dammit," Kennedy said, "I can't sit here while everybody fights the fight I'm supposed to be making. What kind of man do you think I am?"

"There's no other way," Hunter said. "You have to stay here."

"And let the police come and arrest me, I suppose?"

"Exactly." Hunter grinned. "That'll *prove* you had nothing to do with the statement."

Kennedy threw himself into the chair behind the desk. His eyes stared at them moodily.

"Let's go, kitten. Tim."

Kennedy made one last try. "Dammit, Hunter, listen here—"

"No, you listen. If I want a bridge built, I'll call for you. But this is my racket. You tried to handle it by yourself and loused it up pretty good. So—let me take it from here."

Kennedy watched them go. As they left, he slammed his fist down on the desk.

They went down in the freight elevator. As they reached the car, Hunter said, "Get behind the wheel, kitten—you're driving. Blake—you beside her. I'll sit in the back." He turned to Tim. "That dame you were telling me about, go get her now."

"Chuck Byron's girl, you mean?"

"That's the one. Tell her I'll pay her. Get her to me. I don't care how—*but get her!*"

Tim nodded. "And where will you be?"

128

"I'll be getting Blake's statement. We'll go to his apartment."

"*Blake's?*"

Hunter grinned. "You think Mike would ever think of looking for us there?"

12

BLAKE'S PLACE was heartily masculine. Hunting prints hung on the oak-paneled walls. Nicely carved horses' heads sat on leather-topped endtables. There was even a silver-framed, autographed photo of a champion boxer. It all spoke of plenty of money.

Peg Wyatt went into the kitchen and came back with an icebag full of cubes. Blake put it to his face while he listened to Hunter outline the situation.

Hunter spoke tersely. The power of Mike Wyatt had to be broken. Blake's knowledge of the fraud would be an important weapon. Blake had to tell what he knew.

"And if I don't?"

Hunter leaned forward. "Then I'll kill you," he said simply. "Right here and now, I'll kill you."

Blake looked into the slim detective's thin face. He stared into the frozen blue eyes. He saw the twisted straining fingers. He said, "I'll talk."

"Good."

"What do you want to know?"

Before speaking, Hunter turned to Peg. "Better start taking this down."

She poised her pencil above the notebook.

Hunter said, "The city was robbed on the Belt Boulevard job, wasn't it?"

"Yes?"

"Of how much?"

"About seven hundred and fifty thousand dollars."

Peg looked up in surprise. Hunter said: "What about the split?"

"Three ways."

"Which three?"

"Wyatt, the mayor and myself."

"Wyatt and the mayor, eh—even after their falling out?"

"They never got that angry at each other."

"How was it arranged?"

"I certified the estimates of work done on the basis of which payments were made to the contractor." He hesitated, smiled. "I . . . er . . . exaggerated."

"What did Barclay get out of it?"

Blake decided to put the icebag to his nose before answering. "He got paid for the work he did."

"And he turned the excess over to you?"

"Each month. I distributed it to the other two."

"He didn't make anything out of the deal, then?"

Blake shrugged. "Conscience."

"He gave away all the other money, you know that?"

Blake avoided Hunter's eyes. "Conscience," he repeated. There was faint contempt in his voice.

"How did you force him to go along on the deal?"

"Wyatt . . . had something on him."

"What?"

"I don't know."

132

Hunter tried to meet the engineer's eyes. Blake avoided him.

Hunter said: "What did *you* have on Barclay?"

Blake opened his hands. "It was Wyatt—"

Hunter sprang up. He clamped his hand on Blake's shoulder. Blake rose.

"How did you crack Barclay?"

"But I tell you—"

Hunter snatched the icepack, slammed it against Blake's stomach. It knocked the breath out of the man. He doubled over.

Hunter stared at him. He said, suddenly: "It was through Barclay's daughter, wasn't it?"

Blake covered his face with the icebag.

"You bossed the junk racket and she was on the stuff."

Blake said nothing.

"Naturally, he didn't want the word to get around about her. So, you threatened him. Maybe he held out. Maybe you had to cut off her supply to show what would happen to her . . . how she'd fall apart. After that, he'd probably do anything."

Hunter went back to his chair, sat down. "She knew you were blackmailing him. She knew why he committed suicide. That's why she said she'd killed him." He turned to Peg. "You getting all this, kitten?"

She nodded. There was momentary silence while Hunter collected his thoughts. "Another thing," he said, after a minute, "who knocked off that chemist Westrope?"

Blake looked up in surprise. Peg Wyatt lifted her pencil and looked at Hunter. Hunter turned to her quickly. She turned back to her notebook.

"I never killed anyone," Blake insisted.

"You're really the virtuous one. You don't know a thing.

133

do you? How about last night at Mike's place? All you did was turn on the tap for that bloodbath."

Blake shrugged.

"Who killed Westrope?"

"Mike, I guess. I don't know."

"Did he kill Williams, too? And Malbin?"

"I guess so. I don't know."

The phone rang. Hunter put a handkerchief over his mouth and answered it.

"Hunter," Tim yelled at the other end.

"Speaking."

"I found her."

"The Duval dame?"

"She's dead. Shot."

Hunter cursed under his breath. "Where?"

"I just found her in her room. She's in bed."

"Who else knows?"

"No one. What do I do?"

"Just a minute. Let me think." He stared at Blake, at Peg Wyatt. He turned to the phone. "Call Homicide. Give the word to Grogan. No one else—only Grogan. Stick near the place—but don't let yourself be seen. I'll be down to pick you up. Where is it?"

He wrote the address down as Tim dictated it. He hung up and turned to the others. "I've got to go," he said slowly.

Peg said nothing. A gleam of hope lit Blake's eyes.

Hunter went over to the engineer. "I can't take you with me. But, by God," he grinned wolfishly, "I'll fix it so *you* can't leave." He slapped his open hand across Blake's face. "Get up," he snapped.

"But—"

"Get up!" He had the gun in his hand again. He raised it as he would a club.

Blake jumped up hurriedly.

"Move!" He prodded the gun at Blake's neck.

They went to the telephone. Hunter gestured him back, then picked up the instrument and dialed a number.

Blake and Peg stared at him uncomprehendingly.

Eyes on Blake, Hunter spoke into the phone. "Hello . . . I want Mike Wyatt . . . no, no one else, only Mike himself . . . tell him it's about Jim Blake . . ." He pursed his thin lips as he waited.

"Hello . . . Wyatt? Hunter, Peter Hunter . . . yes, I thought you'd remember me . . . I just wanted you to know I found Jim Blake . . . yes, Blake . . . he's been very cooperative . . . told me all about the three-way split on the Belt Boulevard pitch . . . yes."

"Why am I telling you . . . ?" Hunter laughed grimly. "Because I want *Blake* to know . . ." the cold eyes lifted to the engineer . . . "that, if he lets you catch him, he's a very dead duck. But *very*."

Peg said, "You've signed his death warrant."

"Unless he cooperates." He smiled sweetly at Blake. "You will stay here until I get back, won't you? You see," his voice sharpened, "your only hope to stay alive now is if we lick Mike Wyatt."

Blake tried to talk, could say nothing.

Hunter said: "Mike will comb the town for you."

Blake found his voice. "I'm *staying* here."

Hunter frowned. "I hope for your sake, you do."

He went out.

Kitty Duval had lived in a neighborhood of rooming houses. The sun, shining brilliantly, made them look older, dustier, even shabbier than he had remembered them. Hunter slowed the pace of the car. His eyes searched every pedestrian, scanned every idler.

135

He came to the street Tim had given him, swung the car into it. Two police prowl cars were parked in the middle of the block. He cruised by slowly, looking at the house from the corner of his eye.

Tim Moloney was lounging on the corner beyond. Hunter speeded up slightly. He turned the corner, continued until he was certain the police could no longer see his car. Then he slid gently to the curb and waited.

The skinny blond climbed in. Beads of perspiration stood out on his forehead like transparent pebbles.

Hunter threw the car into motion. It moved ahead slowly. "Tell me about it," he said.

"She was lying down in bed when she got it," Tim said. His tone was casual. Elaborately casual, as if he was determined to keep it that way.

"Bullet holes in the bed?"

"Yeah."

"What else?"

"In the blanket that covered her. Cotton thing."

"Sheet, too?"

"Only one and that underneath. I couldn't see."

Hunter stole a sidewise glance at his partner. Tim's face was set. He stared straight ahead.

"Whoever it was," Tim said, "she never had a chance. She didn't even know he was there."

"How do you make that out?"

"She was in bed."

An old peddler turned his banana cart into the path of the car. Hunter swerved to avoid him. "That doesn't follow —I mean, just 'cause she was in bed."

"There was a dressing table. Cheap. Cosmetics on it. Her false eyelashes. A blonde rat. Stuff she wouldn't want seen."

"It figures."

136

"She must have been asleep," Tim said. A tremor quivered deep in his voice.

A traffic signal turned red. The car stopped. Tim said, "Her back was to the door. Arm under her head. Shot in the back."

Hunter waited quietly.

Tim's tongue tried to moisten dry lips. He squeegeed the perspiration off his forehead with a trembling finger.

"I went 'round to the other side of the bed. Lifted the blanket." His voice was tight as a fiddle string. "She was . . ."

"Naked."

Tim's voice cracked. "It's not the first bare breast I ever saw."

The light turned green. Hunter started the car. "Only the first dead one."

"I felt like a peeping Tom. She was so loose, relaxed. Like a goddam ghoul, I felt." He shivered, turned to stare at Hunter.

Hunter kept his eyes glued to the road ahead. His knuckles, as his hands gripped the wheel, stood out white, like a picket fence.

"No signs of a struggle?"

"None." Tim had his voice under control now. "No powder singe on the blanket either."

"What else?"

"Nothing else."

"You got hold of Grogan?"

"Yeah. It took a bit of pulling to get him to the phone. Then he wanted to know who was calling. I hung up on him. They got here about ten minutes before you did."

"They spot you?"

"No."

137

Hunter said, "We might as well go back to them."

He made a U-turn and drove back. The prowl cars were still parked before Kitty Duval's house. Hunter drove up the street and stopped opposite them. Grogan started across the street toward him before he could even make a move to leave the car.

The huge, boulderlike detective walked stiffly and his granite face was grim. "Glad you dropped by," he said heavily.

"You don't show it."

"Okay, boy, so I'm a bum actor."

"You're not even trying."

Grogan lifted a hamlike hand. "What brings you out here, boy?"

"What do you think?"

"I got a stiff inside there." He jerked his head at the house.

"Maybe it's a coincidence," Hunter suggested humorlessly.

"If you look around a cell in an hour and find yourself inside, that'll be more than a coincidence." He turned on Tim suddenly. "Who're you?"

Hunter cut in. "A friend of mine."

"Dammit, I'm not asking you," Grogan growled. He went back to Tim. "Give."

"All right," Hunter conceded, "he's the guy who called you."

Grogan ignored the remark, continued to glare at Tim. Tim said, "That's right. I called you."

"At least, I recognize the voice. Now, lemme hear the story." He glanced at Hunter and paid tart tribute. "I'm sure it'll be good."

Hunter said, "Thanks," drily. To Tim, he said, "Give it to him. All of it."

Tim told of his hunt for Kitty Duval, of how he had

138

traced her from the bar, Spero's, finally dug up her address, of finding her in her room, dead.

"What'd you want her for?"

"I wanted her," Hunter said.

"Why?"

"About a guy named Williams."

"We found his body."

"I read about it."

"Why'd you want this girl?"

"She was at Spero's the night Williams disappeared."

"That all?"

"What else?"

"Every time I find a stiff," Grogan said heavily, "I find you hanging around like a buzzard. Williams . . . Westrope . . . and now this dame."

"Maybe I'm a fatal presence."

"It's not a fatal presence I'm thinking of. It's a fatal touch."

"*That* I am saving for the right people."

Grogan sighed ponderously. "All right, what's your alibi?"

"I was with a friend."

"Who?"

"I can't tell you."

"I'm still asking: Who?"

Hunter looked down at his stiff, groping hands and shook his head slowly.

Grogan swore under his breath. "Son," he said, "I've given you lots of room to romp. More rope than anyone ever got. But—if I don't get some dope soon, I'm going to start pulling the rope in. When it gets real tight, you'll find yourself choked."

"Not me," Hunter said. "I'm like a fish. I breathe through gills."

"Then we'll have a fish fry."

"I wouldn't fry good."

"Too tough?"

"Too many bones."

"Talk," Grogan growled. "All I ever get from you is talk." He reached through the car window. His hand rested heavily on Hunter's shoulder. "Make up your mind. Here and now. Do I get all the dope?"

"And if you don't?"

"I'm going to run you in."

Hunter opened his hands in surrender. "I'm licked," he admitted. "I can't afford to get locked up. I have to be loose to finish things up."

"Start making sense."

"Jim Blake's my alibi. But don't ask me where I have him." Grogan scowled. "Why not?"

"I want to keep him on ice for a while?"

"He stinks?"

"To high heaven. But he's got the inside info I want."

"What info?"

Hunter's fingers beat a rapid tattoo on the wheel. "Enough to blow this town wide open. The Belt Boulevard job. The junk racket. The dirty politics. Lots more."

"Take me to him," Grogan said.

"Not a chance."

Grogan leaned forward, deadly earnest. "Look, boy— either you take me to Jim Blake—or you're coming along with me. And—after I lock you up, I'll turn this town upside down and find him."

Hunter's hands flopped over, palms upward. Tim's eyes widened in shock. He had never seen his partner plead for anything before.

"Grogan," Hunter said, "lay off. Don't play the heavy cop with me. I'm down to the wire. I'm cracking this thing. But I need time. I need a day."

Grogan shook his huge head.

"A few hours then, Grogan."

"No!"

Hunter stiffened. "All right, then, you damned pig-headed dick, I'll take you. On one condition."

"No conditions—take me."

"If Blake corroborates me—and you know damn well *he's* no bosom buddy of mine—you won't pinch him."

Grogan studied the other's strained face. "I probably won't, boy." He sighed heavily. "I'll probably end up kicking myself from here to the morgue. But I'm pulling for you so hard . . ."

Hunter grinned. "You'll brag about this—

"Yeah, I know. To my kids someday. Or they'll be visiting their old man in the pen."

The burly detective went over to dismiss the prowl cars. He came back and squeezed into the front seat with Hunter and Moloney.

At Blake's place, he was first out of the car. Hunter started to follow. Grogan reached across Tim and grasped his arm. "Never mind, son," he said. "I'll manage alone."

Hunter tried to throw the arm off. Grogan tightened the grip. "Wait for me, boy. I won't double-cross you. I'm on your team. But I want to do this my way. And I don't want you there to coach."

Hunter leaned back against the seat. "Go ahead."

Grogan was back in five minutes. His big round face was clouded and deep in thought. His eyes were granite hard.

Wordlessly, he opened the car door and got in. "Start driving, boy," he said. He slammed the car door shut. "I'll tell you when to turn."

Hunter's eyes narrowed. "What gives?"

"You heard me."

Hunter turned off the ignition switch, took the key out and put it in his pocket. "What did Blake tell you?"

141

"Get going, boy."

Hunter stared at the big detective. He began to speak and the slow hysterical bitterness of despair was in his voice.

"I should have known better than to trust you, Grogan. I should have known you're no better that all those other cheap punks, that you've lived with them so long that you'd end up pimping for them, too. I should have known—"

Grogan flung out his heavy boulderlike hand. It slapped across Hunter's mouth, knuckles first. Hunter's head rocked back against the seat. Blood oozed out of a split in his lip.

"Boy, how much of this can a man take?" Grogan asked softly. "How long do I have to swallow your brand of sour pap?"

"I had him, Grogan," Hunter said savagely. "I had Jim Blake. Nailed down, I had him. And he was talking. Spilling his rotten guts. Until *you* butted in."

Doubt seeped into Grogan's hard gray eyes. "Hunter, what do you want?"

"I want to purge this town. I want to cut the corrupt cancer out of it. I want to talk to Jim Blake because he's the knife I have to use. I want—"

"Boy," Grogan said softly, "you'll never talk to Blake. Not ever."

Something in his voice made Hunter suck his breath hard. The mobile fingers stiffened in midair.

"Because, boy," Grogan looked deep into the younger man's eyes, "Jim Blake is dead up there."

142

13

THEY WERE back in Blake's apartment now. In the bedroom. Grogan had been reluctant to return. Now he sought to compensate for the concession by watching Hunter very carefully.

Hunter stood over Jim Blake's body, looking down. The engineer had been shot in the back of the head. The bullet, delivered at close range, had splintered the skull.

Hunter's lips were tight and thin. He swore with soft intensity as he went through the dead man's pockets.

Grogan said, "Just like the Westrope job. Small caliber. From behind."

"A carbon copy."

"Tell me again, boy. You're sure he was alive when you left?"

"Oh, no. I bumped him myself. 'Cause he was my star witness. 'Cause I needed him. 'Cause he was giving me everything I needed."

"How do I know he was talking? Maybe he was going to say you were off your trolley. Maybe that's why you clammed him for good."

Scorn distorted Hunter's laugh harshly.

"Where's the Wyatt girl?" Grogan demanded.

"I'm shielding her. You ought to know that." He began to search the apartment.

"What're you looking for, boy?"

"How the hell should I know? I'm just looking."

He found nothing. He went back to the dead man's wallet. "Plane tickets to Mexico City. A reservation for tonight. Only two hundred bucks in cash." He frowned.

Grogan said, "Where d'you suppose Kennedy's been all afternoon?"

Hunter went to the phone. Kennedy wasn't in the office. He wasn't at his hotel. Hunter turned to Grogan. "You better find out when they arrested him." He offered the instrument.

Grogan took it, called his office, spoke briefly, hung up. "Half hour ago," he said. "They picked him up at his office."

"Half hour ago, eh?" Hunter looked soberly at the bedroom where the body lay. "He *could* have done it."

"A tight fit—but he could have."

Hunter shook his head thoughtfully.

"Kennedy's your white hope, isn't he, boy?"

"I don't think he did it. Still . . ."

"You figure Wyatt for this one, too?"

"Who else?"

"Maybe the girl."

"Maybe Santa Claus, too."

"What happened to her? You said she was here."

"Maybe Wyatt knocked her off, too."

"Maybe."

"Boy, I'm beginning to puke on all this secrecy."

"I can't tell you what I don't know, Grogan. She's gone—that's all I know."

Grogan led the way back to the living room. "All right,

144

boy," he said, "tell me it from the beginning. He lowered his big body into a deep chair. "First, where did you find Jim Blake?"

"At Kiki's."

"Kiki's."

"Sure. He was the man and the money behind her junk kick."

"Then you brought him here. And, you say, he talked."

"After I *persuaded* him, he talked."

"What did he say?"

"There were three in on the paving split. Blake, Wyatt and Mayor Burkett. The take was seven hundred fifty grand."

Grogan started a low whistle. The sound broke off when he heard a soft knock at the door.

The big detective sprang to his feet, revolver drawn. Muscles tensed, Hunter opened the door a tiny crack. A figure in blue catapulted into his arms. It was Peg Wyatt, sobbing and laughing simultaneously.

"Peter." She dropped her huge pocketbook. Her arms tightened around his neck. "Oh, Peter, Peter—I'm so glad. I was afraid. So afraid." She clung to him.

He disengaged himself slowly. "Jim Blake is dead," he said.

Her eyes closed. She swallowed hard. "I know."

"Grogan thinks I killed him."

She turned to the big detective. "He didn't," she said simply.

Grogan's eyes bored into hers. "Did *you?*"

Her "No," was barely audible.

"Kennedy?"

"Oh, no!"

"Your Uncle Mike, kitten?"

Her breasts rose in a long reluctant sigh. "Yes," she whispered.

145

"It was horrible," she said softly. "Jim had finished giving me his statement. I had typed it up and he had signed it. Then, as I was witnessing it—"

"What happened to that statement?" Hunter asked excitedly.

She picked the big pocketbook off the floor where it had fallen. She opened it, took the rolled cylinder of pages of legal foolscap from it. Hunter's fingers snatched it a split second ahead of Grogan's clutch.

They devoured it with hungry eyes. Hunter looked up at Grogan who was reading over his shoulder. Hunter's eyes shone. "The McCoy, eh Grogan? The works. I've got 'em now."

Grogan's big face beamed. He clamped a pulverizing grip on the younger man's shoulder.

Hunter's face sobered quickly. "I'm sorry, kitten. Tell us the rest."

"Right after I signed, Uncle Mike burst into the apartment. He was furious. He had a gun in his hand." Her eyes closed and a look of pain and fright came to her face as she seemed to re-envision the scene.

The words kept coming faster and faster. "Mike said: 'Get the hell outta here and keep your yap shut.' I held my bag so that it covered the statement and ran out. Even through the closed door I heard him storming at Jim. Calling him a rat and a squealer. I started to run down the stairs. Then I heard the gun—" her voice stumbled in its headlong flight. "That must have been when . . ." She stopped, unable to continue.

There was silence until she recovered. "I didn't know what to do. I didn't know where to go. Then I remembered Mr. Kennedy was waiting at the office. I went there. But he wasn't in."

Grogan cleared his throat, a rumbling thunder of sound.

146

"I kept walking. I must have walked for miles. Then I found myself back here again. Mr. Moloney was downstairs in the car. He told me you were up here. I came up."

"You did well, Miss Wyatt. Very, very well." Grogan patted her hand. He looked at Hunter. Suddenly, he snapped: "You happy, boy?"

Hunter nodded. Reluctantly.

"Then how come your eyes don't smile?"

Hunter turned away from Grogan's probing eyes. "I don't have Mike yet, do I? It doesn't count until then."

"Is that all, boy?"

"What else?"

"I wish I knew."

As though deliberately changing the subject, Hunter said, "What are you going to do now? Will you go after Wyatt?"

Grogan hesitated. "On what basis? A dead man's statement. It isn't enough."

"What about Peg's testimony about Wyatt killing Blake?"

"It's her word against his."

Hunter said: "I see."

The big man wiped the palm of his hand across his moon-like face. "See here, boy—I can't go up against Mike on the basis of what you've got. He'd eat me up alive."

"We've got everything now." He lifted his outstretched fingers, checked them off as he made each point. "We've got an eyewitness—Peg. A motive—to choke Blake off. A reason —the paving mess."

"But you can't make any of it stick."

Hunter extended the taut fingers as if they were the probing antennae of an insect. "There's too much killing. The setup's so saturated with blood that some of it has to seep through somewhere."

Grogan said, "The leak'll have to get bigger than this piece of paper."

147

The angular fingers tightened to a fist. "Close your eyes for six hours, Grogan. I'll widen the leak into a canal."

"I haven't seen a thing, boy. I don't know a thing." He gripped Hunter's shoulder. "I hope you put it over. I'll be rooting for you."

It was past seven when they rode down in the elevator. Grogan reached for the Blake statement which Hunter carried.

"I know a place I can have it photostated," he explained. He told Hunter the address.

"It's not that you don't trust me?"

"You'll find the original waiting there for you."

"And you won't take a copy?"

"What do you think?"

He left them there. Tim came out of the car and Hunter outlined the situation briefly.

Tim's eyebrows climbed up his forehead. "How did Mike Wyatt know where you had Blake?"

Hunter said nothing.

"D'you suppose Kennedy could have told him?"

"It's possible."

"We may still be backing the wrong horse."

"That's possible, too."

"You're not going to tell me too much about this, are you?"

"No."

Tim yawned ostentatiously. "Well, if there's anything I can do to help—by all means, just ignore me."

"Get those housing vets together. You'll need them tonight. It's going to be rough from here on in."

Tim nodded.

Hunter turned to Peg. "Look, kitten, walk ahead to the restaurant. I'll catch you in a moment."

He waited until she was out of earshot, then said: "She'll have to be guarded every minute until this thing's over."

148

Tim gasped. "You figure something might happen to her?"

"It's a cinch Mike is not going to let her live to testify. Get those boys. Put a stake-out at her apartment. Pick up any one of Mike's yeggs who tries to get through. I don't give a damn what you do with 'em." He walked away, hurried until he'd caught up with Peg.

He couldn't conceal his tension at dinner. He talked constantly to Peg, loosely, like a drunk on a talking jag. His expressive hands were in perpetual motion as he launched into a description of the ambush of Kiki's forces. Vividly, he described the burning house, the wounded man moaning out on the pitted lawn.

"It was like a scene from your Robinson Jeffers poet," he said. "You know: 'Life is a midge-dance of gutted and multiplied echoes.' "

Her eyes were fascinated. Her lips were curved in an enigmatic smile. Her voice was cool and remote. "And 'Death's like a little gay child that runs the world around with the keys of salvation in his foolish fingers.' "

" 'Lends them at random where they're not wanted,' " he finished softly, " 'but often withholds them where most required.' "

She shivered. "Peter, when will it all end?"

"End?"

"The murders. The bloodshed."

"When the killers get theirs."

She shivered again. "And when will that be?"

"Who knows? Tonight, maybe."

"Tonight!" Her lips parted, her eyes widened. "You'll be careful."

"I'll try."

"If anything should happen to you . . ." Her eyes filled with tears.

149

He said, harshly, "God, you're beautiful."

She shook her head, avoided his eyes.

He said, "You look a million miles away. Unreachable. Like a star—" He broke off sharply and stood up. "It's eight-thirty. I have to pick up those photostats. Powder your nose and wipe the worries from your eyes. I'll come back for you in five minutes."

When he got the copies of Blake's statement, Hunter mailed the original to himself, care of general delivery. The others he folded and put in his breast pocket.

Peg was waiting at the table when he returned, her makeup restored. Her eyes were clear but the smile on her face was subdued. They left immediately.

At Peg's house, a man came out of the shadows toward them. Hunter paused momentarily as he approached. If, during the slight hesitation, he saw the man's faint nod, he gave no sign, made no acknowledgment of it.

At her apartment door, he stopped. "This is as far as I go, kitten."

Her hand clutched his arm. "No, Peter, no." She clung to him, almost desperately. "I'm . . . frightened."

"All right. I'll come in."

She sighed her relief. He could hear the noise she made as she swallowed. He put the key in the lock, flung the door open and waited. In the silence, the expiration of her breath was clearly audible.

"See? Nobody. Nothing." He pretended to heave a sigh of relief. "I'd probably have fainted."

Her giggle had overtones of hysteria in it. "I'm a coward, I guess." She led the way inside. "I just can't help it."

He watched her fiddle with the cap of her enormous pocketbook: watched her try to moisten dry lips with her tongue; saw her bite hard on her lower lip.

150

He said: "You'll feel better when your conscience is clear."

She turned to him. There was shadowy fear in her eyes. She walked to him, sagged down beside him on the sofa. Her shoulders slumped.

He took her hand. It was cold as ice.

She said: "I . . . lied."

"To me?"

"And Inspector Grogan."

He waited for details.

She rose abruptly, went into the bedroom. He heard a drawer open, then shut. She came out with an envelope. She handed it to him.

Hunter opened the envelope. It held one hundred dollar bills. Twenty of them.

Hunter looked up. "That's an intriguing color, kitten."

"Uncle Mike didn't just chase me this afternoon. He gave me those. To keep quiet."

"So?"

"I can't keep them."

"No?"

Her eyes widened. Her hand went to her mouth. "Why do you torture me, Peter?" she cried. "You know there's blood on that money."

"It's your headache." He handed it back to her.

She took it with nerveless fingers. The envelope fell from her hand to the floor. Revulsion contorted her face. She stared at it as though it were a snake.

He picked it up, threw it into her lap. "You should have told Grogan," he said stiffly. "It would have proved something."

"I was afraid."

"Afraid?"

"You don't know Uncle Mike."

He stood. "After tonight, maybe there'll be nothing to fear."

Horror darkened her eyes. She clenched her fists. "You're going to Mike now!"

He met her eyes. He nodded.

"You mustn't!"

"Why not?"

"Because he'll kill you."

Disdain twisted his cruel mouth. "Is it me you're worried about, or your precious uncle? Is this why he gave you the two thousand dollars? To hold me here?"

Her eyes were tortured pools of tears. "If I could only make you *understand!*"

"What's there to understand?"

Her arms went around his neck. He tried to force her away. She clung to him, pressed her body hard against his. He reached behind his neck, unclasped her hands.

She said, "If I thought my body could hold you here—"

"It couldn't," he snapped.

"I'd do it willingly." Her head was high, her eyes met his without shame. With pride and dignity.

"I'm going," he said stubbornly.

"It's not myself I'm afraid for," she told him proudly. "It's you. I wouldn't want to live without you. You've no right to risk leaving me alone, to gamble your life."

He said, grimly, "This is a new approach."

"You don't understand. I've never been afraid of death for myself. But for you . . ." Her voice choked, trailed away.

"I'm different?"

"Why do you persist in misunderstanding me? Why do you close your mind?" Her voice was anguished.

She sat down hopelessly. His eyes followed her. He watched the sigh rise from the depths of her being. His eyes

152

went to her breasts. Though small, they seemed to swell against the confines of her dress.

His eyes were slightly bloodshot now. He fought to swallow an obstruction in his throat. He put his hands to his ears to shut out the throbbing in them.

He looked into her eyes. That sense of infinite depth, of bottomless beyond conception, conveyed itself to him. The veins in his forehead stood out marking the struggle within him against going to her.

But finally, he moved toward her. He sat down, put his arm around her. She turned to him. Their eyes met. His face went over hers, his lips went to hers.

His arms tightened. He pressed hard against her; his body forced her body against the back of the couch.

She disengaged herself and turned her face from him. "Haven't you known, from the beginning that it was different? Don't you know it now?" Her voice was soft, insistent. "D'you think I'd beg anyone else?"

He took her hand, pressed his lips to it.

"I've spent my whole life running away from my uncle. Until tonight. But now I've stopped running. From myself as well as from him. I've found the courage to look into myself."

She turned to look at him. His smile was boyish.

"Until tonight," she said, "death held the fascination." The emotion she found to suppress underlined the words, made them tremble. "Death was inviting: it offered freedom. But now there's *you* . . . and life is something to hold onto . . . the future is something to look forward to." Her voice held a sense of wonder. "And dying—dying is something to *fear*."

Hunter closed his eyes. He turned his head away.

"In *that* house,"—he knew she meant Mike's—"the world was sordid. It was a refuse for vice and the vicious. Gunmen

153

. . . addicts . . . gangsters hiding from the law. Some nights I had to share my bed with prostitutes." Her grip on his hand tightened. "When I was fourteen, a madam pinched my breasts . . . told me she could use me soon. Uncle Mike laughed when I told him."

The tears refused to stay dammed up any longer. They rushed out and, as though ashamed of them, she hid her face.

Beside her, Hunter sat rigid, body hunched, face stiffly expressionless. But the long, eloquent fingers betrayed the inner compulsion. They started toward Peg in a wavering line.

But the gesture was never completed. In the middle of it, the thin fingers stopped: the jaw squared; reluctantly, the fingers drew back. Like a man wrestling with a heavy weight on his back, Hunter strained to his feet. The effort whitened his face.

She lifted her head. Her mouth was parched. Her voice cracked as she said, "You're going anyway?"

"I'm going."

She opened her hand in defeat. "I knew you would." She said: "Your life is in danger. It always will be. Until you go so far from here that you can no longer threaten him."

"You want me to run away?"

"Yes."

"With you?"

"Yes." She breathed the word like a prayer.

"I can't."

"Why do you go to him?" she asked wonderingly. "Do you *want* him to kill you?"

"I have no choice."

"You don't love me?"

The expressionless granite façade of his face cracked.

154

The quick biting acid of pain flowed through, etched deep sears into his mouth.

"This is no night to talk of love," he said. "No, nor even think of it." His face had set into hard lines again. His eyes were cold and bleak. The thin electric fingers reached out: stiff and curved and predatory.

She lifted her hand, palm up, in an eloquently importunate gesture. Now, she saw it was useless. The hand fell away with the laxness of defeat.

She covered her face with her hands. The door slammed shut but she didn't even look up.

She began to cry . . .

14

DOWNSTAIRS, he stood before the building. His eyes stabbed up and down the street. Tim Moloney detached himself from the shadows of the building and hurried forward.

Hunter said, "Well?" brusquely.

"They came."

"How many?"

"Four. Two right after you came. Half hour later, two more."

Hunter cursed aloud.

Tim said: "Mike is really anxious to get her, isn't he?"

"He doesn't take chances. Where'd you take 'em?"

"The vets have 'em."

"Good."

"Will Mike keep trying for her?"

"Until her funeral."

"We'll keep watching then."

Hunter shook his head irritably. "She's not safe. Not up there. One of 'em might slip by. Got to get her somewhere else."

157

Walk the Bloody Boulevard

"Okay. Where?"

"Get Grogan. Tell him to take her in. Book her as a material witness. That'll keep her safe for tonight, anyway."

"And after tonight?"

"After tonight there may be nothing to fear."

Tim lifted his head. "You're going after Wyatt now?"

"Right now."

"Keep your finger on the trigger. He's treacherous."

"Okay, okay," Hunter said irritably. "Here's what you do. First, make sure Grogan has the girl safe. Then, go to Kennedy's office. Search it. The private office. There's a lot of dough lying around there. Probably in a suitcase. And look for a gun, too. A small caliber."

"Kennedy's!"

"That's what I said."

"You think Mike planted the stuff there?"

"I'll explain later—when I know what it's all about myself."

"I'll be listening."

Hunter turned to go. Tim grasped his shoulder. "Hey, wait—lemme tag along. Just for laughs."

"No. It's a one man job. *My* job."

Tim squeezed the shoulder convulsively. "Give Mike all my worst."

Hunter's grin was as sharp as an icicle. "And that ain't all!" He moved off into the darkness.

It was a low, two-story brick building. From the roof down to the level of the first story, there hung a huge portrait of a benign face. The gigantic red letters beneath it read:

MICHAEL J. WYATT POLITICAL ASSOCIATION
All Welcome.

158

Walk the Bloody Boulevard

Peter Hunter stood in the darkness across the street from the building. He stood there and watched the lights inside go out. The weekly, free-admission Saturday night dance had ended. The teen-agers who, in a few years, would be voting with their friend Mike Wyatt, had already trooped out. Now, the last musicians left, accompanied by a motley half-dozen hangers-on.

Now, the windows in the big meeting room were dark. A single bright light burned in the rear of the building, indicating that someone was still working in the office.

Peter Hunter looked down at his watch. The luminous hands looked like two fat little lazy worms. They said it was eleven thirty.

He took a last long drag at his cigarette, then threw it to the ground. His foot stamped hard on the glowing butt. He looked up and down the street. It was empty.

He crossed the street, moving quickly, yet without giving the appearance of hurrying. He turned into the alley that paralleled the building's side. Under a window, he stopped.

His eyes slitted, seemed to stab through the darkness. He saw no one, heard nothing.

He reached up. The wire strong fingers secured a hand hold on the window ledge. He hoisted himself up, poised there.

His hand reached up, sought to push the window open. It refused to budge. The hand went into his pocket, came out with a blue-steel bladelike tool. He inserted it into the window catch. There was a low but distinct snap.

He waited for a full minute on his perch. No sound disturbed the silence. He pushed the window up. It slid quietly. He twisted himself through the open space. His feet, when they made contact with the floor, made a faint thud.

He stood in the darkness, breathing hard. The big meeting room was empty. Folding chairs were stacked against the

159

wall. Yellow light seeped under a door at the rear of the building. Hunter moved toward it.

It was warm. He stopped to wipe the perspiration from his forehead, then leaned his ear against the door. He heard nothing. He stood on the balls of his feet, lips moving in wordless curses.

He put his hand on the knob, turned it and walked inside. At the sound of the door closing, Mike Wyatt looked up.

He was sitting behind a desk and, when he saw Hunter, he nodded as if this was something he had been expecting. The paralyzed face remained stiff as stone, but satisfaction gleamed in the yellow green eyes.

"I knew you'd come, Hunter," he said conversationally. "I've been waiting for you."

Hunter's smile was careless. "I thought you would."

"You've been busy?"

"You know I have."

Mike's lips quirked in the abortive smile that ended at the corners of his mouth. "The boy Hercules, cleaning out the city's Aegean stables."

"I hope you'll be as unconcerned when you're flushed away."

"Don't hold your breath."

"I won't. I'll shut yours off."

He watched Mike's fingers inch beneath the desk. His eyes narrowed but he said nothing. After a moment, Mike's hands came into view, empty.

Hunter said: "I came down to persuade you to confess. It will save everyone lots of trouble."

Mike's laugh was pre-occupied. His eyes went to the door behind Hunter before he answered. Finally, he said, easily, "But there's nothing to confess."

Hunter put his hand into the inside pocket of his jacket. The politician's yellow green eyes widened, showed fear.

160

Hunter laughed at him. "That's the trouble with you cynical guys," he said. "You can't see a man put his hand into his pocket without thinking he's reaching for a rod."

His hand came out holding the photostatic copy of Blake's statement. He threw it onto Wyatt's desk.

Wyatt glanced at it. There was a low sound outside the door. The yellow green eyes flicked toward it. Hunter heard the sound and, instinctively, his head started to turn toward the door. In the middle of the gesture, he stopped.

By an effort of sheer will, he ignored the danger developing behind him. He kept his attention glued to the politician before him.

Wyatt picked up the photostat. "Interesting," he said, turning a page.

Hunter's voice was taunting. "You never expected it, did you? You thought you'd fixed Blake beyond singing, didn't you?"

The yellow eyes darted to the door again. The sound of a footstep outside was more distinct now. Mike began to talk very loudly to cover the noise outside.

Hunter heard the ratchet of the door knob as it turned. His fists clenched in the effort required to pretend to ignore it. His shoulders hunched involuntarily, as though trying to protect his head from the imminent assault.

Mike was almost yelling now. "Underestimate you . . ." he was saying. There was a frantic note in his voice.

Hunter heard the door open but he did not turn. Then the gloating wheeze of Chuck Byron's voice blasted at his eardrums.

"Pray, wise guy—your party's over," it exulted.

Hunter closed his eyes. He sucked his breath sharply.

"No!" Mike yelled.

Hunter waited for a moment that lasted an eternity. Then he saw Mike nod and knew Byron had obeyed.

161

Hunter closed his eyes. He swayed dizzily. The sucked-up breath whistled out through his nostrils. The tortured fingers relaxed.

"Lemme drill 'im, boss," the hoarse voice pleaded.

Hunter turned to look into Byron's eyes. Fever burned in them.

"I could have been dead before you got here," Wyatt snapped.

"I didn't hear the buzzer, boss. I was asleep upstairs."

Wyatt turned to Hunter. "You see, I *was* prepared."

Hunter said, "I saw you press the button under the desk."

Wyatt started a smile. "Come now—" He broke off the patronizing statement. As he realized that Hunter spoke the truth, a mixture of surprise and fear clouded his eyes. He said: "So you got a statement from Blake."

"Pretty, isn't it?"

"Where is the original?"

Hunter didn't answer. Mike stared at him as though trying to get the answer by sheer force of will. Hunter met his stare, laughed mockingly.

Wyatt nodded to Chuck. Hunter's laughter stopped abruptly as Chuck slashed at his head. Chuck Byron moved toward him as he fell.

As Hunter hit the floor, the gunman lashed out at him with his foot. Hunter tried to block the blow. The shoe battered through the clutching hands, seared deep into the bruised ribs. He pitched forward, full length.

Mike's eyes smiled. "All right, Chuck. That's enough."

"Lemme finish 'im, boss."

"Chuck!"

Glowering, Chuck stepped back. Hunter got to his knees, pressed his hands hard against the floor, managed to stand unsteadily. His lips pressed hard against each other. His face set. There was no sign of pain on it.

Chuck leveled his gun at Hunter. The ex-pug took up a position of guard, slightly behind and to the right of the detective. The hand that held the gun twitched.

"I am not fooling, Hunter. I want the original of that statement. I'm going to get it."

"Go to hell."

"Lemme open 'im up, boss."

Hunter threw his head back with the air of a man starting a counter-offensive. "What good would the original do you? You're facing a murder rap on this Williams business."

The yellow green eyes measured him.

"We've got all we need," Hunter told him. "Muggsy and Chuck were spotted at Spero's the night Williams went there. We've got a witness."

"You have?"

"You bet. Kitty Duval."

There was oily satisfaction in Mike's voice. "And how do you intend to get Kitty to testify? Will you bring her back from the dead?"

Hunter's hands jumped convulsively. A wild joy flamed in his eyes. "Sure, you know you killed her. And I know it. But—*does Chuck?*"

He stiffened while he waited for the news to penetrate the gunman's thick skull. It took a long moment. Finally, the bewildered wheeze sounded behind him. "Kitty? Dead?"

It was the move Hunter had waited for. While the gunman concentrated on Mike for his answer, Hunter side-stepped fast. He swung his arm stiffly. His braced hand chopped, like the blade of an axe, against Chuck's unprotected throat. The gunman went down like a sledged steer.

Hunter bent swiftly, picked up the gun. He leveled it at Mike. "Come out from behind the desk. Sit in the chair here." He waited for Mike to comply. Then he said softly, "Now, it's you against me."

163

Mike pushed out his chest. "All right, shoot."

Hunter shook his head. "No, I'm not going to shoot."

Mike's eyes shifted to the stricken figure on the floor. "I'm not afraid of that gun," he said quietly.

"I know it. You'd like it. It would suit your opinion of yourself. Going out in a blaze of glory." He smiled. "I'm not going to give you *that*."

Wyatt looked at the gun longingly.

"You see, Mike, you've been a sucker all through this thing. You've been a chump."

The yellow green eyes narrowed. He licked at his lips.

"We're going to begin by pinning a murder rap on you. For killing—of all people—Westrope."

"Westrope!"

"Isn't that ironic, Mike? A big shot like you in exchange for a sordid little smutty-minded chemist."

There was intense quiet while Wyatt thought it over. He tried to laugh. The sound came out but the dead facial muscles locked. The effect of the boisterous sound and the empty features was gruesome.

"I have an alibi," he said finally. "Foolproof. Ironclad. I was with George Kennedy when it happened."

Hunter's eyes mocked him. The detective's voice sneered. "You were *alone* with Kennedy, Mike. D'you think he'll back you up? After you tried to ruin him? To pin everything on him?"

Mike licked at his lips nervously.

"That's another irony, too—isn't it, Mike? The guy you picked because you knew you could jump him through a hoop. And he ends up sending you to the gallows."

The sweat broke out on Wyatt's forehead. He wiped it away irritably.

Hunter went on insistently. "We found the gun that killed Westrope, Mike. You know what it was? Listen to

164

me—this is going to shock you. A twenty-five, Mike. Remember it? A twenty-five. It's registered in your name."

Wyatt stared at him, puzzled. His elbow went to his thigh and he rested his chin on his hand as though too tired to hold his head up. And he kept staring.

Hunter's voice took on a new note. He spoke meaningfully, as though there was more meaning in his words than was openly stated. As if there was a message in them that he wanted the other to figure out for himself.

"Let me put it this way, Mike:. Westrope was pulling out, Mike. He took his money out of the bank. He took his bonds out of the vault. Yet—the money disappeared." Hunter leaned forward. *"Mike—what happened to that money?"*

Mike started, as if he suddenly realized what the other was trying to say to him. Then he shook his head angrily as if unwilling to face the hidden meaning of the words.

"That's ridiculous," he said with obviously assumed disdain. "I've got all the money I need." But his eyes remained far away as he mulled over Hunter's words.

"But you did take the graft on the Belt Boulevard job. I've got a theory about guys like you, Mike. It isn't enough for your to know you're smart. You have to bolster your ego by proving it all the time. By rigging paving frauds and stealing money you don't need. By murder." His eyes were scornful and again his voice became pregnant with unstated meaning. "And—then you end up as a sucker."

"Sucker!" The word roused Wyatt. His eyes smoldered.

"You know what I mean. You're holding the bag for the murder of Westrope. But someone else skimmed the gravy. No, no—don't wave it away," he said as Wyatt made a dismissive motion of his hand. "You know what I mean. I see it in your eyes."

"Burkett wouldn't dare," Mike yelled.

"You can't bluster with me, Mike. Not Burkett. *Burkett!*"

165

Again Hunter's laughter mocked him. "Why Burkett? Who are you trying to fool? Me? Or yourself?"

"I don't know what you're talking about. I . . . I . . ."

"Oh yes, you do." Hunter's words came out with inexorable insistence. Wyatt squirmed under their impact. "You've bungled at every turn. You chose Blake—and what a mistake that was. And now—Peg is going to testify against you."

"Peg!"

"You didn't think she'd keep quiet, did you? That your lousy money would keep her quiet forever?"

"Peg." The name seemed to hold a bitter fascination. He turned it over on his tongue. "Peg."

"You think this is crap?" Hunter hammered on. "Okay, then—check me. Call the D.A.'s office. You'll find she's been booked."

With trembling hands Mike dialed the number. He asked one quick question, then slammed the receiver down. He shook his head groggily. "A material witness—Peg."

He looked at Hunter. His eyes focused on the gun and sudden resolution flamed in them. He threw himself at Hunter's gun hand.

It would have been impossible for the detective to miss him if he shot. But Hunter sidestepped coolly. He batted the gun against Wyatt's head as the politician lunged. Wyatt fell to the floor, lay there.

"That was another mistake, Mike. Did you think I'd shoot you? That I'd save you the humiliation of standing public trial? Of being pecked at by the vultures you made?"

Wyatt beat at the floor with his hands.

"You made so many mistakes, Mike, that it's hard to believe that you were ever smart. You brought in a public prosecutor to frame Kennedy. Now, he's going to get you instead. And you ran to Burkett and showed him how weak you are. D'you think Burkett'll fight for you? Hell no—this

166

is his chance to take over. He'll throw you to the wolves, let you take the rap."

Mike got to his feet slowly. He sat down. His head bent forward. His shoulders slumped. He was beaten.

Hunter looked at the politician. Triumph flared momentarily in the pale blue eyes. But, as quickly as the flame shot up, it died down.

His face became as haggard as Wyatt's. A haunted look came into his eyes. A look of fear. As if he faced a problem that robbed him of his courage.

He tried to talk but his mouth was suddenly too parched to enunciate words. A croaking sound came out. Mike looked up suddenly.

Hunter took a deep breath as if nerving himself for an ideal. His voice came out, painfully soft. "Mike," he whispered, "I'll make a deal with you."

"A deal." Wyatt's eyes blazed greenishly.

"I want all the information. Not just you, but everyone. Every dirty little crook and sneak thief. Every petty grafter."

Mike leaned back. "And suppose I go along—what's in it for me?"

"What do you want? Time off for turning state's evidence? The right to cop a plea? A light sentence?"

"Me in jail? Mike Wyatt sitting in the pen for those punks to laugh at? Coming out a broken old has-been?"

"Then what?"

"I want to go my way."

"Your way?"

Mike fixed his green eyes on the gun, stared at it steadily. "You know what I mean—my way."

Hunter met his eyes, had to avert his own glance. "And you'll tell the whole story?"

Mike shook his head. "I haven't finished with my demands yet. I want more."

167

Hunter waited for him to go on.

Mike lifted a finger. "I want to take someone with me."

"Who?"

"You ought to know. You're the one who called me a sucker."

Hunter swallowed audibly. "Tell me who, Mike."

"Think it over, Hunter. A twenty-five. Registered in my name. *You* know who."

Hunter's lips trembled. His voice shook. "You're asking me to play God. To write the book of Fate. Good God, man," he asked in anguish, "who do you think I am?"

Mike shrugged imperturbably. "That's your headache."

"That's the only way it can be? The *only* way?"

"The only way."

Hunter looked down. His eyes fixed on the gun he held. He shuddered at the sight of it. He clenched his free hand. He stood abruptly, knocking the chair over.

"It's a deal."

15

THE ATMOSPHERE in the cluttered anteroom of the Homicide Division was as tense as an air raid shelter. The air was stale. A dense cloud of cigarette smoke hung in lazy suspension.

Mike Wyatt bustled in, closely followed by Peter Hunter. At the sight of them, Grogan stiffened. His approach was wary.

Tim Moloney came on the dead run. He was carrying a small cowhide suitcase.

Hunter rapped out quick words of command. "Need a private office. A stenographer." He winked. "C'mon along. Mike here has a story to tell."

Mike Wyatt eyed the men in the room contemptuously.

Grogan jerked his head toward a closed door. Hunter led Mike through it immediately. Grogan called a stenographer, followed with alacrity.

Inside the room, Hunter turned to Tim. "You found everything?" His face was grim.

Tim tapped the cowhide suitcase he was carrying. "All

169

there, just as you said. No gun, though." Sneaking admiration showed in his bony face. "You had it figured: he made the plant at Kennedy's."

Bitterly, Hunter said, "Yeah." He turned to the stenographer. "All ready?"

The man nodded, poised the pencil above his notebook. Hunter said, to the others, "Mr. Wyatt here has a story to tell—one that we're all anxious to hear."

"Right." Mike's acknowledgment was crisp and sure. The yellow green eyes had a supercilious gleam. "The best goddam story you ever heard."

They leaned forward. Wyatt looked around the circle of faces, deliberately building his suspense. Finally, he began to speak. Directly, emotionlessly, as though he was recounting a political maneuver to a group of subordinates.

The paving fraud (Mike said) had been born in Jim Blake's brain. Blake had come to Mike and assured the politician of the unbreakable hold that he had on both Barclay and the chemist, Westrope. Since this was before Mike had been estranged from Mayor Burkett, the rest of the deal was quite easy to arrange.

Matters had proceeded smoothly and profitably for all until the job was completed. Then, came the first fly in the ointment: the meddling of Samuel Williams. As soon as he learned of Williams's suspicions, Mike ordered the old chemist picked up. This had been done right after his meeting with George Kennedy.

As they had feared, the old man knew too much. Even though all the tests were supposed to be done by a private firm, headed by Westrope, Williams had arranged to get samples for testing. And, on his person the night they intercepted him, he carried the papers showing the results of his tests. There was no doubt that the old man had established the certainty of fraud.

"And so you killed him?" Hunter interjected quickly.

Mike's lips quirked in an unfinished smile. "I'm not confessing to murder."

"And when Malbin started for the D.A.'s office to tell of how he had given Williams the materials to test, you had to get him too, didn't you?"

Mike regarded him with amusement. "Suppose you let me tell it my way."

He had thought that the knowledge of the firm's guilty involvement would be enough of a check to control George Kennedy. But Kennedy proved obdurate about the appointment of Montgomery. And, in the meantime, Hunter began to make progress in the unraveling of the details of the paving scandal. Therefore, Mike decided the best way out would be to bare the guilty details, but make Kennedy responsible for them.

Naturally, Jim Blake, in hiding at Kiki's, had been kept up to date on these developments as they occurred. (Here, for the first time, bitterness crept into Mike's voice.) And when Mike left for the capitol to persuade the governor to give him a special prosecutor, Blake made the mistake of trying to turn the alleged raid—of which Hunter had informed Kiki—to his own advantage.

Blake arranged the ambush of his own dope gang, hoping thereby to eliminate a number of followers who might prove embarrassing and, at the same time, explain the death of the old chemist, Samuel Williams, as the by-product of a gang war. That done, his decks would be clear and he could skip out.

"That was the big mistake," Hunter interrupted to say. "The connection between dope and paving kept getting stronger. Whoever was behind the dope racket had tried to get me. Why? After all, I had done him a favor by tipping him to the raid. It could only be because of my investigation

171

into the paving fraud. I had decided, by then, that Blake was the crook on the Belt Boulevard paving. It was a strong hunch that he was the dope man, too. That was the only way it made sense."

"Of course, the governor gave me the prosecutor I demanded," Mike continued. "Then I got Burkett, outlined the situation and told the pigheaded fool he'd have to cooperate with me long enough to get Kennedy or we'd all get caught. He agreed. We decided that Blake was to leave the country, leaving behind a statement implicating George Kennedy."

"Would you have let him go, Wyatt? Or killed him after he signed the statement you wanted?"

Mike dismissed the question with an airy wave of his hand.

"Then," Hunter persisted, "you'd make a pretense of standing by Kennedy, but making sure he went down. Was that it?"

"We were going to finish it off today," Mike said. "That's why the special prosecutor arrested Kennedy this afternoon."

"That's why I insisted he stay at the office," Hunter said. "I knew there'd be bloodshed and if Kennedy was in jail when it came, no one could frame him for it."

Grogan spoke up for the first time. "The Blake killing's what I want to hear about." His voice was brutally hard. "It's our best case. We've got your niece to testify against you."

Mike stiffened as though electrocuted. *"Dead!* Blake dead?" The words exploded out of his mouth. He turned to Hunter. "You dirty louse," he said, his voice softly venomous.

"I didn't tell you he was alive," Hunter said drily. "And you'd hardly be talking here if you knew that statement you saw had come from a dead man." He leaned forward. "Besides, it makes no real difference. Peg says she saw you kill him. We've got more than enough to fix you."

172

"You pulled a fast one," Mike admitted grudgingly. His tone was an admixture of admiration and bitterness.

"Thanks."

"But how do I know the rest of the stuff you told me isn't a phoney as well? How do I know I'm not being conned all the way?"

Hunter extended his hand toward Tim. "The brief case," he demanded. Tim handed it over. Hunter held it so Mike could read the initials, "J.B." beneath the catch. "Know it?" he asked.

"Blake's."

Grogan leaned forward to follow the by-play between the two. Distrust narrowed his granite eyes.

Hunter threw the suitcase to Mike. "See for yourself."

Mike opened it, looked inside. He shut it quickly. He turned on Tim. "Where'd you find it?" he snapped.

"Where you planted it. In Kennedy's office."

Hunter took the bag. He handed it to Grogan. "You better take charge of this. There's probably a hundred grand in it."

Grogan looked inside the suitcase and his eyes widened. When he looked up, Hunter and Wyatt were exchanging glances.

"What the hell is going on here?" Grogan demanded hotly. "There's a helluva lot of secrecy and I'm fed up. Is this guy going to confess, or isn't he? And if he is, why doesn't he tell it without all this futzing around?"

"Dammit," Mike flared, "this is my *life*. I can take my own sweet time."

He took a deep breath. Anger and fear and regret and indecision showed in his eyes. And, through the maelstrom of inner emotion, the stony face remained unmoved.

"For God's sake," Grogan exploded, "what—"

"Okay," Mike said.

173

"You'll see it through?" Hunter asked.

"Yes."

"Start talking," Grogan commanded.

Mike made an easy gesture. "I have to see Peg first."

Grogan's eyes went hard. His face stiffened into a concrete slab. "What kind of deal is this?"

Mike's laugh was bitter. "I'm a guy who can get hung, Grogan. I don't talk until I know where I stand. So," he opened his hand, "I want to see Peg."

"Go to hell."

"I can soften these other raps, Grogan. I'll cop a plea. In a couple of years, a pardon or a parole. Then I'm free again. But with the rope," slowly he lifted his hands to his throat and encircled it with stiff fingers, "it's too late for any pardons." He rested his hands on his thighs. "If I don't see Peg, I don't talk."

"No," Grogan insisted stubbornly.

"You want all the dope, don't you, Grogan. And you want me to *sign* that statement after it's typed up."

Grogan hesitated. "It's wrong—"

Hunter stood quickly. "I'll get her. Where is she?"

"Wait," Grogan said.

"Let him see her," Tim said. He pointed to the window. "It's a four story drop to the street. He can't go anywhere."

Grogan shook his head dubiously, then said, "Okay." He walked out the door. The others followed.

Hunter was the last to leave. He stopped with his hand on the knob, turned as though to argue with Mike. Then he changed his mind and left without saying anything.

Triumph gleamed in Mike's yellow green eyes.

Peg was alone in the matron's office when he got there. She closed the book she was reading and looked up at him.

174

He said nothing.

She smiled and her heart-shaped face looked sweetly young and virginal, her lovely eyes infinitely deep. She waited for him to speak.

His hands were strangely still. He stared down at them, at a loss for words.

"Well, Peter," she asked, and her voice had that eerily luminous quality, "what happens to me now? Why did you have me brought here?"

Softly, he said, "Your uncle's been arrested."

The bottomless eyes widened. "Arrested?"

"He's confessed."

"And now you're happy, Peter?"

"Should I be?" he asked bitterly.

"I don't know," she answered gravely:

He said, abruptly: "Your uncle wants to see you."

"See me? Why?"

He didn't answer immediately. Instead, his eyes met hers, held them until the silence became oppressive. His hands were stiff and tight, the fingers curved in strain.

Finally, he said, "Don't you know?"

She asked, "How much do *you* know, Peter?"

"I know it all."

"*Everything?*"

"Everything."

"I wasn't very clever, was I?"

He shook his head.

She sighed like a disappointed child. "Tell me . . . about my blunders."

"The bad one was Westrope. You said he called you at one-thirty—but the medical examiner said he was dead before noon."

"That's why you accused me of lying last night?"

"I thought you were trying to protect Kennedy or your

175

uncle. It didn't occur to me then that you had killed him."

"And when did you realize?"

His smile was almost indulgent. "It came on gradually. I kept thinking back and little things began to stand out. First, after I frightened Westrope at his apartment, he made a phone call to Kennedy's office. Later, it occurred to me it might have been you he was calling."

"Second, the woman's clothes in his trunk. They were the colors a blonde would wear. Third, Mike knew Williams had arranged a secret meeting with Kennedy. Someone inside Kennedy's office must have told him that."

"Mr. Williams's call came to me first. After I transferred it to Mr. Kennedy's extension, I listened in on mine. I heard him tell Mr. Kennedy of the results of his tests. I knew Uncle Mike would want to know about it."

He nodded. "I thought it was that way. Then, this evening, when I took you home, I was convinced. You told us Mike had killed Jim Blake. But, if he had, he would never have let you live to walk out of that room."

"You think Mike would kill me?"

He sobered. "I *know* he would."

She thought a moment. "I imagine you're right."

"There were more tell-tales. Both Westrope and Blake were badly frightened men. They would never have turned their backs on Mike Wyatt. Yet, each was shot at close range from behind. It must have been by someone they trusted. You would fit that bill."

She said, "I was supposed to leave with Mr. Westrope. Had you realized that?"

His jaw tightened. "I told you I saw the clothes in his trunk."

"I meant to go."

Bitterly, he said, "But you changed your mind and killed him?"

176

Her eyes stared off into space. A spasm of pain crossed her face. "I don't know why. It was a sudden thing. It just came to me that what he was running away from, most of all, was himself. And that he could never escape." Her voice softened. "I did him a favor. He's better off now."

"And *you?*"

"I thought I would take his money and go away."

"It didn't occur to you that you were running away from yourself."

"Not until later." Her eyes filled with sudden tears. "I've always lived in a prison. Fighting to get away."

"And that's why you killed Westrope? And Blake?"

"Yes."

"And yet—you didn't go."

She lifted her face to him. "Don't you know *why?* Because I wanted *you* to come with me. I suddenly found someone I needed. Someone I loved. And when I asked you to run away—you wouldn't come."

"You didn't really expect me to, did you?"

"Not really. No, deep down, I knew I would never have you."

"And that's why you tried to have me killed?"

"Poor Peter." Her hand barely touched his cheek. "Yes, I called Mike while you went to get the photostat. I told him Blake had broken down and you had his confession. I told him I would try to bring you to my apartment." Her voice became pitiably tender. "Do you hate me for that, Peter?"

His smile was wry. "If you had succeeded, I would."

"You knew what I was doing?"

"I wasn't sure. I just figured I ought to protect myself against the possibility." His voice grew bitter. "Y'see, I hardly felt like offering myself up as a living sacrifice to your love."

She said, "I'm glad you escaped," and her voice was sin-

177

cere. Self disgust warped her face. "It's always been that way. Feeling imprisoned. Doing horrible things. Regretting them later. Detesting myself." She covered her face with her hands. She did not cry, but her body trembled with the sobs she suppressed.

He stood and began to pace the office. "And then you tried to push everything off onto Mike, didn't you?"

"Don't you see," she pleaded, "why I did that? It would make you happy if Mike were broken. And it would give me a chance to have you."

"Over your uncle's dead body, is that it?"

Hands shaking, he lit a cigarette. He sucked smoke deep into his lungs, expelled it violently. He began to pace the office again, striding with a certain nervous explosiveness.

"You'll have to pay," he said suddenly. "There's no other way."

She opened her hands in fatalistic acceptance. "How?"

"If you stand trial, you'll get life. Maybe less. Certainly, no jury would hang you."

"Life—in prison?" There was horror in her voice.

"What else?"

"To sit there . . . alone . . . in four walls . . . with only my thoughts. To grow old without living." She lifted her head. "And that is better than the death sentence?"

He crushed the cigarette with slow gravity. "Your uncle wants to see you."

Her lovely eyes narrowed in bewilderment.

"I told Mike we'd traced the gun to him. I was sure it would be the one you told me he bought you. I figured he'd get you a light thing, a twenty-five. And that he'd have it registered in his name when he bought it."

"But I don't understand."

"He thinks the owner of that gun made a sucker of him. He wants to get even."

178

For a moment she didn't know what he meant. Then, like the sun coming from behind a cloud, a dazzling radiant smile of gratitude covered her face. "I'm so glad, Peter."

"I knew you'd want it that way. That's why I told him, baited him. Until he sold himself for the right to get even."

"You did it for me, Peter." She went to him, reached out her arms to embrace him.

He put stiff hands against her breasts, held her off. "No more of that."

Tears sparkled in her eyes. "I'm trying to thank you."

She leaned forward on tiptoe. Her lips brushed his. She stepped back. "See? That's all."

Their eyes met, locked hungrily. He seized her arms, pulled her to him. Her open mouth went to his. His arms tightened until it seemed he must crush her.

Finally, he flung her away. "You'll be dead soon," he snarled. "*You* won't have to remember."

Her lovely face was soft. Looking into her eyes was like staring deep into the infinite.

"There is no other way, is there, Peter?" she asked in a whisper.

His eyes devoured her. For a moment, it seemed he would take her and run. But then he squared his shoulders. He shook his head.

"No," he said, and the word seemed to have been wrenched from his very soul. "No, there's no other way."

He took her hand. Together they walked down the empty corridor. The sound of their footsteps resounded from wall to wall. The echoes made Hunter feel that his insides had evaporated, that his skeleton was nothing more than an empty frame.

She stopped to listen to the echoes. Her face lifted to his as she smiled painfully, twistedly. "Is someone walking on my grave?"

179

They walked on. His face had set stiff as cement. It was the face of a man on his way to face a firing squad.

They entered the anteroom of the Homicide Division. Detectives, lounging there, turned to look at them. Grogan said, "Where the hell were you?"

As if he hadn't heard, Hunter turned his back, shielded the girl from Grogan's eyes with his body.

She pointed at the office where Mike waited. "He's in there, Peter?"

He started to speak but his mouth was too parched to bring forth sound. He nodded, fearfully.

She said, "Thank you, Peter." Her hand rested lingeringly on his arm. As if she wanted her last contact with life to be with him.

He turned away. The doorknob ratcheted as she turned it. The sound made him close his eyes.

She whispered, "Good-bye, Peter," and the sound, barely audible, boomed in his ears like a thunder clap.

The door closed.

Hunter turned to find Grogan staring at him distrustfully. The ponderous head cocked to a side like a boulder poised at the edge of a cliff. The huge body stiffened, suddenly hurtled forward.

"I'm going in there," Grogan thundered.

He charged at the closed door like an enraged elephant. Hunter crouched to meet the avalanche of his body, then threw himself at the big detective's knees. Grogan was knocked sprawling.

Hunter tried to crawl on top of him. A ponderous swipe of Grogan's arm knocked him flat to the floor.

"You crooked louse," Grogan roared. "I'll break—"

The sudden crack of a gun behind the closed door cut his words off. The shots followed in slow, evenly spaced, terrible cadence. One . . . two . . . three . . .

180

Walk the Bloody Boulevard

The shots ceased. There was silence.

The knob turned slowly, as if a clutching hand clung to it. Then came the dull thud of a falling body.

Another shot. Another thud. Then . . .

Silence.

16

AN HOUR had passed, and now Peter Hunter sat in another of the Homicide Division's offices.

He sat slumped over and there were haggard lines in his face. His weariness was like that of combat fatigue, a complete and total exhaustion of all the physical and psychic resources.

The thin lips, usually so hard and cruel, were soft and relaxed now, as if his will had lost the power to clamp them against each other. The cold blue eyes were shadowed and haunted.

And the hands—the wiry, electric, ever-moving eloquent hands—lay drooping and limp.

His head sagged forward and he looked at the floor as he said, wearily, "It was the only way. The only possible way."

"If you say so, that's good enough for me."

Hunter flashed a small, grateful smile to his partner. "Thanks, Timmie. Thanks."

George Kennedy said, "It's all so incredible."

The engineer had been released from his cell after the

183

tempestuous excitement had died down. Now, his clothes were disheveled and there were deep shadows under his eyes. He no longer looked boyish. There were new, older lines in his face, as if, during this night, he had gained a storm-induced maturity.

"Poor Miss Wyatt," Kennedy said soberly, "I'll never understand why—"

"Let's forget about her," Hunter snapped roughly.

Tim stared hard at his partner. Hunter turned his face away as if he feared the scrutiny.

"All I wanted to say," Kennedy persisted, "was that I never felt sorrier for anyone in all my life." He shook his head wonderingly. "Does that surprise you? It does me."

"I'm sorry," Hunter apologized. He drew a deep breath and deliberately changed the subject. "How does it feel to be about to become mayor?"

"I owe that to you," Kennedy admitted. "In fact, I owe my very life to you."

Hunter smiled wryly. "Just pay me that bonus and we'll call it quits."

"Gladly."

"All's well that ends well," Tim remarked drily.

Grogan appeared. He stood glowering in the doorway, reluctant to enter. Finally, he moved in and sat down.

"A clean sweep," he told them heavily. "We found everyone of those guys Mike had told you about. All the petty grafters and the chiselers." He turned to Hunter. "That Byron was still laying on the floor in Mike's office. You must have hit him quite a clout. He can't talk yet."

"I was afraid I'd killed him. I'm glad I didn't."

Grogan rumbled on. "The honorable Mayor Burkett was on his way to the airport to keep a date with a plane. He'll be no trouble."

Kennedy said, "I hope I do better than he did."

184

Grogan said, "Congratulations, sir. It looks like you're my new boss."

"Hunter's been telling me I ought to make you my Chief of Police." He smiled teasingly. "You might as well be the first to know of your new appointment."

Grogan held back. "I'm not sure I want it."

"No?"

"I'll want a free hand. No interference."

"Of course."

"If you're sure you want me . . ." The big detective's smile was unconvincing, his reluctance obvious. Finally, he turned to Hunter and said, "I'd feel better if I didn't owe it to you."

Hunter said, "Think nothing of it." He tried to sound flippant, but it came out weary and flat.

Tim took Hunter's arm. "Let's get the hell out of here," he said. "This is one lousy victory celebration." He lifted his partner to his feet.

Hunter stood there, swaying slightly. He started to speak, then closed his mouth. His eyes were dull, his face gray.

Grogan slammed his fist on the table, shattering the silence. "Dammit, boy," he thundered, "you're not that big. Setting yourself above the law. Maneuvering people like chessmen. Twisting them so that they kill each other."

"That's a helluva way to talk," Tim said angrily. "The guy cracks your case, cleans your town and you give him lip. Where the hell would you be if it weren't for him? Digging your head in the sand and making believe you didn't have to bow down to the petty chiselers and racketeers. You ought to keep your big bazoo shut."

"All right," Grogan agreed ponderously, "so they both deserved to die, Mike and his niece. And maybe we wouldn't have been able to convict her. But the place for people to be sentenced to death is in the courts. Not in some private

185

eye's mind." His voice softened as he addressed himself to Hunter, but was no less insistent. "Son, you had no right to play God."

Hunter smiled wearily. "Funny, that's exactly what I told Mike." He took Tim's hand off his arm, and stood free. "I had to decide. Either to give Mike his way and clean up the mess—or let them go free. What would you do?"

He tottered, put his hand on the table to steady himself. The pain in his ribs showed in his face now and he made no effort to hide it. "As for Peg—would you say she's more dead now than she would have been in a prison cell."

He turned his haunted eyes down to his hands. The long thin electric fingers trembled. By an effort of will, he stilled them. They seemed to soften, relax.

"Grogan," he said softly, "No one ever felt less like God than I do."

A spasm of pain warped his gray face. His shoulders slumped and his head sagged forward.

He turned his back and walked out.

THE END

186

www.ingramcontent.com/pod-product-compliance
Lightning Source LLC
Chambersburg PA
CBHW030336180626
46810CB00003B/1380